# INTIMATE
# DISASTERS

# INTIMATE DISASTERS

by **CRISTINA PERI ROSSI**

Translated by

**Robert S. Rudder** and

**Ignacio López-Calvo**

Latin American Literary Review Press, Pittsburgh, Pennsylvania 2014
Svenson Publishers, Claremont, CA 2018

Acknowledgements:
This project was supported by the Pennsylvania Council on the Arts,
a state agency, through its regional arts funding
partnership, Pennsylvania Partners in the Arts (PPA).
State government funding comes through an annual appropriation
by Pennsylvania's General Assembly.
PPA is administered in Allegheny County
by Greater Pittsburgh Arts Council.

PENNSYLVANIA
COUNCIL
ON THE

**ARTS**

Library of Congress Cataloging-in-Publication Data
Peri Rossi, Cristina, 1941- author.
[Desastres íntimos. English]
Intimate disasters / by Cristina Peri Rossi; translated by Robert S. Rudder
and Ignacio López-Calvo.
 pages cm
ISBN 978-1-891270-54-3
I. Rudder, Robert S., translator. II. López-Calvo, Ignacio, translator. III.
Title.
PQ8520.26.E74D3913 2014
863--dc23
2014041117
Cover art by William C. Jones        Book design by Jennifer Lahmers

# Table of Contents

# FETISIHISTS, INC.

On Saturday evenings I'm the only woman at the Fetishists Club. All the other members are men.

We get together on weekends, before Sunday, dumb Sunday, the most miserable, gloomy day. Sunday is a day that's battened down: reality hangs over everything, without hope, without adornments, in other words, without art. At most, you can sleep a little longer, along with the noise from the neighbor's shower, the elevator packed with kids (children are on the loose on Sundays, and nobody knows what can happen with all that explosion of hormones), or the telephone that's always ringing to announce the ritual visit of the in-laws, a forgotten anniversary, or the illness of a great aunt who, among other things, is eighty years old. The weight of reality, that's what Sunday is: when a person has absolute proof that the apartment is too small for four people, that the lack of space gives rise to (or exposes) hostility, that you can eat paella or baked lamb, that if you go to the movies with your husband you feel alone, but if you go to the movies alone, you feel alone.

That's why we fetishists prefer to get together on Saturday, at dusk. Saturdays, in contrast, seem to be days filled with possibilities, with fantasy, with hope. On Saturdays some people dream about a man or a woman who will stir up an unknown passion; other people dream of a nighttime journey through the subterranean underbelly of the city (what is wondrous is never on the surface, you have to submerge yourself to find it; the wondrous is peripheral, marginal, hidden, a tunnel, a sunken world, a region in limbo), some think they're capable of writing a book, and others, of winning a fortune at gambling.

We fetishists make up an anonymous society, just like alcoholics, or compulsive gamblers. We're a secret society, the way others could be formed: men with small penises, a society of lefties, short people, ex-seminarians or admirers of Robert Redford. To be addicted to slot machines, alcohol or panties, to be an ardent admirer of Robert Redford, to collect all his photographs, videos of his movies, and be madly in love with his discreet little pouts, seems a lot more important to me than a person's job (one that he quickly gets bored with), or the family you belong to, made up of three or four people who detest each other, although they pretend not to, who fight over money, space and affection, like vultures. Because the relationship that a person establishes with his fetish (whether it's black nylon stockings, the bells on a machine bustling with lights, or a glass of whiskey) is always personal, non-transferable, solitary and intense. That relationship is the most intimate thing we have, the most authentic place of our subjective self.

At first there were four of us, but then the group grew. We put a limit on it: only twelve of us fetishists get together at a time. New people who want to become members have to form their own club. We call ourselves the founders, the first generation. The people who belong to this original cell include Fernando, a civil engineer; José, an office worker; Francisco, a photographer; and

6

myself—the only woman—, my name is Marta, I'm a teacher and I live alone. Who else could I talk to about my passion for men's necks—only their necks—if not to Roberto, who collects women's black patent leather shoes—the ones for the left foot, or José who adores brassieres, or Francisco, the photographer, who would lay down his life to be able to photograph a pair of "lazy-eyes." A woman's, naturally: he has absolutely no interest in the strabismus of men. "I don't even find the right eye of a cross-eyed person tantalizing on those klutzy, clumsy men's bodies," says Francisco. The same thing happens to me with necks: I'm only attracted to male necks; female ones—I can't bear to look at them. *Not all necks*: just some. Not even necks that are similar: sometimes I'm mad about a long, slender neck, with the shape of a pine tree, those necks that stretch to the heights and make you think that the person who has it is a dreamer, a romantic creature; but other times I'm irresistibly attracted to a neck with a prominent Adam's apple, sticking out like a penis with an erection. No man with a prominent Adam's apple can hide his condition as an erectile animal, first biological, then spiritual. In those cases I think I love the contradiction between instinct and culture, between the being that slobbers, sweats, defecates, gets sick and snores when it's asleep, and the imaginary construction: a being who feels, thinks, speaks, makes choices, buys a Fiorucci tie, listens to a Brahms sonata.

We all have a secret, then. Having a secret is a very burdensome thing. When I fell in love with Fernando, for example, how could I explain to him what I felt? Fernando was thirty years old and he wanted to get married, "to start a family," as he said. He was working somewhere: I don't remember doing what. Oh, yes: at a bank. He always knew a lot of things about loans, taxes, stocks and all that. He was proud of his ability to handle money, to make investments, that sort of thing. When he showed how proud he was of his abilities, I laughed out loud and he got offended. He accused me of not really being interested in his life. Very true (I couldn't tell him that): all my interest—an enormous amount, by the way—was concentrated on the involuntary, completely unconscious way his Adam's apple would go up and down, all by itself. His Adam's apple stuck out, and I gave it all my attention. No matter what he was talking about (in general, men's conversations seem completely irrelevant to me: they talk about business, politics or soccer as forms of self-assertiveness, in the most absolute and demanding way, all in order to build up their egos), that Adam's apple went up and down, rhythmically, somewhat pointed, the flag or symbol of things that have no name, things I still didn't know, or perhaps that he didn't know himself.

"When it comes to the things that people tend to talk about, I'm not interested in talking about them," I told him.

"You're crazy," he answered me, very sure of himself.

Men really like to think, or to think they think, that we're crazy. We're crazy just because sometimes we won't accept the things they say, or we're crazy when we don't want the same things they do.

"For more than two thousand years, psychology and psychiatry haven't been able to define madness," I answered him, even at the risk of having his Adam's apple

8

disappear from my view, "but you, on the other hand, can diagnose insanity so easily. Bravo."

I liked to rattle him. When I got him rattled, his Adam's apple went up and down faster. But I couldn't tell him that either: it would hurt his ego. He wanted me to love him for his competence at business (pardon me, bank management), for his wish to have a legitimate family and all that.

I lost his Adam's apple once and for all the day he knocked at my door without letting me know he was coming, and I opened it innocently, thinking it was somebody selling shampoo or the man who reads the gas meter. The building's intercom was to blame—it was broken—so I opened the door, not knowing it was Fernando. We always made love in his bachelor's apartment, or at some hotel whenever he gave in—grudgingly—to my penchant for making love in unfamiliar rooms.

My reactions are slow, so when Fernando came in, it didn't cross my mind that he was going to be so astonished at the collection of photographs of men's necks that I had, scattered around the dining room and the bedroom. Other people have pictures of ridiculous little men wearing short pants, with T-shirts and badges, insignias and things like that.

"What are these?" he asked, looking at those photographs in their frames as if they were something disgusting, sickening, full of pus and disease.

Lordy, I don't think it's all that hard to recognize that they're necks. That's all: just necks. Don't people have their houses full of photographs of faces? Actresses, singers, the grandmother, the aunt and the cousins. And a lot of them dead, to boot.

"They're photographs of necks," I told him softly, prepared for the worst.

Now it was time for Fernando to try to make me feel guilty. The battle of the sexes goes like this: the one who makes the other person feel guilty, wins. Men have it the easiest because they've been doing just that for thousands and thousands of years.

"And why are you keeping all these stupid photographs?" he said to me.

"Some people collect stamps, or butterflies or coins. I collect necks," I explained, matter of factly.

He looked horrified.

"You mean to tell me that for you, men are objects for some hare-brained collection?"

"I don't see anything odd about it," I countered. "People have photographs of their mother, their children or their girlfriends, and it doesn't cross anyone's mind that it's the same thing as pinning a butterfly into a display case. If I had a photograph of my father or my grandmother, instead of necks, I would find my apartment just plain depressing. And I live in it," I declared.

He moved among the photographs nervously, as if he would grant me the privilege—for the moment—of taking my arguments into consideration, of weighing them, while he was making up his mind whether to condemn me or forgive me. I thought that if he found the necks seductive enough, he might consider me innocent, but it was a weak hope: seduction is something that is very, very subjective, and he certainly wasn't capable of distinguishing one neck from another.

As it happened, he picked one up by the frame and

examined it, and then another, and he asked me in sheer amazement:

"So, are you trying to tell me that each of these necks is different, and that you can see the difference?"

"Just the way you can tell the difference between every vagina and every face," I went on the attack, for once.

He put it back in its place on the mantel, and shook his head doubtfully (his Adam's apple went up and stayed there, as if it would never come down again. I had an anxiety attack when I thought of that possibility).

"I think you're crazy," he declared.

He'd already told me that before.

"Have they all been your lovers?" he went on.

"No," I told him (I held back the word "unfortunately").

"How did you get all these photographs then?"

I know from experience that the pleasure we fetishists feel when we narrate all the problems, inconveniences and obstacles we've had to overcome to get one of our favorite objects (that black silk brassiere with satin trim that was only worn once by the woman who never gave in to us, or the pink panties of the neighbor lady on the third floor, that hang somehow innocently on the clothes line, in view of the whole world, as if they were really just one more article of clothing, inoffensive, lacking any significance at all except that of covering part of her body) is incomprehensible to everyone else. It makes up part of that secret that is our subjective self. That, the thousands of vicissitudes, the sacrifices we've had to make to get hold of the object of our desire, only another fetishist can appreciate. The coveted panties, the neck gazed upon so avidly would mean nothing to another person. Because it's *the look* that gives it its value. A superficial glance, which is the most common one, is not able to detect, on the four-pence Queen Victoria stamp, pearl number twenty-six on the oval border, which makes it a rare, limited item, because the great majority of four-pence stamps with the image of Queen Victoria only have twenty-five. In the same way, Fernando could not see in all the photographs of necks scattered around the room, anything more than that: necks, all very similar, Adam's apples. But that was a superficial look, stripped of symbols, that skimmed over the surface without ever seeking the mirrored image.

"Some of them are from magazines. Some of the others, I took myself."

He looked at me in astonishment.

"And you would really cut a photograph out of a magazine just for the neck?" he asked me.

I wasn't sure if he asked the question simply out of curiosity, or if there was some hidden reproach in it. I was capable of not only that, if he really wanted to know: for a long, full-bodied neck, with large, open pores, and with a wide, smooth nape (like Down's syndrome), I'm capable of a great deal more. For the delicate, beautiful, white neck of an adolescent boy, creased with blue veins, like rivers on a map, I'm capable of more than you can even imagine, Fernando. Once I had to suffer through two hours of conversation about a soccer game just for the possibility of biting into a sumptuous, round Adam's apple, large enough for me to choke on, feel it go down my esophagus and pound against the walls of my stomach.

"It looks to me like you're a fetishist, and that

12

you're not right in the head," muttered Fernando.

Now that was a notable advancement, for him to say, "it looks to me like," and not to decree categorically, "you are." It was an indication that he had lost some of his customary self-confidence. At the point where doubt begins, that's where you can begin to talk.

According to psychological treatises, fetishists take the part for the whole: a foot, the eyes, the breasts, a piece of clothing or an object represent the whole, and they feel a sort of mystical adoration—like the faithful before the divinity—for that part or that object. We read that definition at the club, and we felt that it was partially in error: for us, a part (the left foot covered with black patent leather shoes of Roberto, or the lavish brassieres collected by José, or the wandering lazy-eye that Francisco photographs obsessively) does not *represent* the whole, it *is* the whole. For the majority of necks that I have loved, I have loved only the neck. For example, let's talk about Fernando himself. Fernando had a lovely neck: lissome, even, with delicate texture, and in spite of all that, you could easily make out the veins and tendons. When he got excited, the tendons tensed up, as though the force of his emotions could be transmitted through them. Alongside the involuntary expressiveness of his neck, everything else was irrelevant. I was able to isolate his neck from the rest of his body, from the rest of him as a person, perfectly, and madly love its warmth, its form, its color, its structure. It was no less a love because it was directed specifically at his neck. Why should I love him more if I spread that love among his other parts?

Francisco, the photographer who loves crossed eyes, says that love is a secret, because the loved one

13

wants to be loved for certain things that don't coincide with the things loved by the lover. He had fallen in love with Julia, a lady with lazy-eye, who suffered bitterly from an error of nature that she had not been able to cure. He had sat before her for long hours at a time, utterly entranced by that strabismic look (erratic, Francisco called it) that strayed from its object and did not stay fixed, like a lost wanderer, like a traveler gone astray. While he contemplated her in solitude ("All pleasure is solitary," says Francisco), Julia told him about her life, her feelings of inferiority at school, the way her companions mocked her, the anguish she felt at being different, how difficult it was for her to have personal relationships. Francisco paid only scant attention to what Julia was saying, because he was fascinated by that eye, that lone lost eye. Aroused by his own love, he was emboldened to say, "But I love you just because of your erratic eye, your wild eye." Julia felt very hurt, and thought he was making fun of her. Humiliated, angry, she accused him of not being able to love her because of her condition. Julia refused to see him again, and Francisco fell into a deep depression. He wanted to see that straying blue eye again, that lost, childish eye that slipped uncontrollably over the chairs, over the carpets.

A secret is very burdensome, and that's why we got together as a club. It's easier, together, for us to talk about pleasure, absence, deprivation, seduction. For example, José came to the meeting on Saturday, absolutely shaken: the evening before, at home, with his wife and his two little girls, he was watching a television show from the U.S., one of those trite, hackneyed ones, when a scene suddenly left him absolutely stunned: in order to bottle-feed a baby, a man was using a sort of huge, artificial, plush bosom, hanging around his neck, and on it were two large breasts, each with their respective teats where the milk flowed through. He had never seen anything like it (he thought the Americans, as usual, were very advanced), and he suddenly felt jolted: *Why hadn't he thought of that before?* An object like that must have been lying away in his fantasies for years. At the club we immediately set about helping him take the proper steps to have the object of his desire materialize: we wrote letters to stores in New York, asking for it, and we got in touch with the TV channel so we could rent that episode of the program.

All us fetishists know that the object of our adulation is the one that exists today, as well as another one, a very old one, submerged in the history of the ages. Necks, for example. Why was the guillotine invented if not for the fact that the neck is really the symbol of sex? The end-purpose of the guillotine was to sever the head from the body, but what is really cut is the neck.

In the club I can say something I never confessed to Fernando: when I look at a masculine neck, I immediately imagine the relationship it has with his sex. There are broad necks, rugged ones, with a big base, like a bull's, that you can expect no more from than brute sex, without imagination, endowed only with force. I, on the other hand, prefer the slight necks of adolescents, very fair, warm, in which the Adam's apple seems to be an unstable object, as if it were suspended in a dream. The neck joins our animal part—the body—to the most ethereal part, the head. But that union, the path that goes from the basic organs—heart, liver, spleen—to imagination, isn't always realized in a harmonious way.

15

There are necks that are too long for the head they hold up: they show that the head wanted to separate itself disproportionately from the body holding it up. And there are necks that are very short, squat, non-existent: the head seems to be buried in the shoulders, without any separation. These are generally rustic, primitive, unsophisticated people.

Fernando told me that all those necks scattered throughout my apartment made him nervous: "There's something missing from them. They're missing the head." He felt like he was surrounded by amputees, or something like that. While for me, on the contrary, the necks were complete. They didn't need much more: the imagination could fill in the rest.

From that moment on, he began to feel that I was watching him. "I don't feel comfortable," he said. "I get the sense that you're performing a clinical examination of my neck." He was wrong: I would never examine anyone's neck like that. A neck can be loved, admired, sucked, bitten, caressed, dreamed of, slurped, licked or kissed, but it can never be examined clinically. Fetishes are not objects of investigation, but rather of love. They belong to the sphere of faith, never of science. That's why I prefer men who shave with a straight-razor: I like to lick those tiny drops of blood that appear, like bursting flowers, from parts hidden to our eyes. Fernando began to shave with an electric razor. It doesn't leave any traces behind. Spotless. Discreet. I could only lick up a little soap or lotion.

I would have preferred to go on making love in his apartment or in hotels, but he insisted that he wanted to get used to mine. It seemed to me that he meant he wanted to

16

get used to the necks. I didn't like having him there, not one damned bit. It was something we didn't need to share, like the way you don't need to share reading the newspaper, or arguments with your mother. Every once in a while I caught him looking, all by himself, at those necks, as if he wanted to discover something hidden.

"It's useless," I told him. "Nobody can see what another person sees."

Maybe those words were what made him leave. Because he went away forever.

"I feel like all those necks are looking at me," he told me.

How odd. I know that I'm a fetishist, but until then I hadn't realized that he was a little bit paranoid. Necks aren't eyes, Fernando: they're sex organs.

# THE WHITE WHALE

"She's fat, and big as a whale," said the little man, his eyes wandering, as though searching along the cold space of the wall for the shadow of the white cetacean on the restless surface of the waters.

"Smooth and sleek too, like a whale's body. Have you ever noticed that whales don't have hair? They're bald," he declared confidently.

The roads of Eros are unpredictable.

"I've never spent much time whale-watching," I said softly, although I didn't think my remarks would make much difference to the little man.

In fact, I didn't think he even needed an audience: he spoke out loud, for his own ears, and that's the best way to listen to yourself. It's normal for men or women who talk out loud to themselves to feel ashamed, as if they're crazy; that's why some men or women have to pretend they're speaking to a listener, but that's only for the sake of appearances.

"It's not the first time this has happened to me," explained the little man, answering a question that I hadn't asked. "When I was young—I'm forty now," he declared, "I fell in love with another woman who was shaped like a whale, but with dark skin: a blue whale. Anyway," he added, "it was an imperfection."

Eros is subtle: any man or woman whose central nervous system is stimulated by the current of love (like a feverish beehive), develops an extraordinary ability to use metaphors. But no one knows—not even they, themselves— what they are describing. The object of their desire remains invariable, resistant to analysis, to words that attempt to capture it, the way a hunter in a forest pursues the fleeting shadow of a deer, a puma, or perhaps an optical illusion brought on by heat, humidity, the hour of the day, and fatigue.

"Why was the dark skin of that first woman an imperfection?" I asked him with feigned innocence. "There are blue whales too— you've admitted that."

It seemed to me that the little man had become aware of me for the first time, he was accepting me as a listener.

"Blue and white aren't loved the same way," said the little man. "Sometimes," he added, "if you love the white, you don't love the blue at all. If you would go out on the ocean," he continued, "you would see that fishermen and harpooners can distinguish a blue whale from a white one perfectly."

These similes sounded extraordinary to me, coming from a man like this, born and bred on firm ground, whose feet were used to traveling the grey, unremarkable sidewalks of the large city. I thought the little man must also be startled that Eros should awaken such associations and images in him, and that he had no idea where they came from.

"In some way that I can't fully comprehend," he continued, "I find their enormous size fascinating (Did I tell you that she's big and fat, like a whale?): and their hairless skin too. In a certain sense," he added, "it's as if I'd found an ancient archetype of beauty, although that word is ambiguous, and ambiguities make me uneasy."

The little man turned in his chair, as though the uneasiness he had spoken of had reached down into his body, into his lower limbs, his shoulders and his long bones. I asked myself if this uneasiness was only due to the inadequacy of language (exactly that, when he was making the greatest effort to be precise), or if the unease, without his realizing it, was a result of his having come across "an ancient archetype of beauty," as he had said before. Then I thought that it was neither one or the other: it was both. I also thought the little man was on the verge of making that discovery.

"It's strange for me to talk like this," he said, as if, for a moment, rationality should be trying to impose itself over the profusion of images that were erupting from he knew not where. "At forty years of age," he added, "sitting in a bar, passing the time, describing the effect of a woman's body on me—one that some people would call obese—, and that no one but myself would say is beautiful. In a way," he quickly added, "it troubles me that others don't see what I do in her, and this leads me to believe that I'm half-crazy. But on the other hand, it seems to me that my eyes are sharper, more intelligent, and if other people can't see what I see, it's because they're myopic or not paying attention. There are very few times when we stop to *truly* look at other people," he insisted, "because the masses are boring, they're not stimulating at all."

I thought that never again during his lifetime would that little man possess this lucidity of mind. In some indescribable way he had come upon a sort of revelation, he was dumbfounded and fascinated, as if the revelation had overwhelmed him, but he would rise above himself by means of it too.

"Sometimes I have fantasies," he confessed, nearly ashamed. "For instance, I imagine that I'm walking down the street, with the whale by my side, held by a rope. The image captivates me…"

"It's very curious that the *captivation* (you hold her by a rope) is turned against you…" I interrupted.

I thought some part of the little man's amorousness (some part of his brilliance and energy) had touched me too.

"You're right," admitted the little man. "I hold onto her as if I were the master, but I'm the one who is captive. Without taking into account the fact," he added, "that whales don't walk, and that they aren't land animals."

"Imagination takes no notice of reality," I tried to help him, "and perhaps it only gives shape to our most primal desires."

The little man turned again in his seat.

"I've tried to analyze that fantasy," he said. "It's struck me that I may have a desire to put it on public display, in the street. To be seen, to be noticed by everyone…"

"An odd pair," I observed aloud. "A small man, with a white whale walking at his side as if it were a dog."

"No, replied the man. "Nobody could compare her to a dog. She is very dignified," he explained. "She's never like a submissive woman. Whales are only subdued when they're dead," he said. "Only after a mob of greedy, cruel men are able to pull it, badly wounded, on board, does it submit. The essence of my fantasy (walking down the street with her at my side, on a leash) is more one of exhibition than of subjection. I ask myself, why do I feel a need to exhibit myself, although I know that I want to put myself on display with her—not alone. We would be a curious spectacle," he remarked, as though to himself, "a small man with such a large woman."

"Perhaps," I ventured, "being loved by such an enormous woman gives you a kind of satisfaction."

"She takes up the whole space," insisted the little man. "Sometimes, at the movies, I have to help deposit her in her seat."

"*Deposit?*" I asked.

He listened to my question as though he were slightly annoyed.

"Since I've fallen in love with her, I've become very precise in the way I speak," he said. "Because of her size she doesn't sit down like everyone else: she spills out over the seat or she *deposits* herself in an armchair with great difficulty."

"Do you like to help her sit down?" I asked.

For the first time the little man, who always seemed to be engrossed in thought, smiled, and a look of pleasure swept over his face.

"Oh, yes," he exclaimed very excited. "She is quite large," he insisted. "Her body, her corpulence takes up a lot of room. She has to be very careful with her proportions, with her relationship to space. Sometimes the doors are too small for her, she's too wide or too tall, the beds in hotels are too narrow, and in the car I need to move the seat back. I have to take care of all these things that I'd never thought about before. Now, understand me," cautioned the little man, "I've had other loves in my life. But they have always been normal women whose weight

22

and height corresponded with what doctors advise. And those women were very happy to be that way. Moreover, if they gained weight, they went on a diet and exercised so that they would look thinner. Have you ever noticed how unimportant people's bodies are in normal relationships?"

I indicated some doubt about that.

"We're only concerned with our bodies at times of intimacy," explained the little man. "Afterward, our bodies go their own way, separately, autonomously, and they become nearly invisible. This intensifies the isolation of each of us," he said. "Is anyone concerned about *his own* body while he's out walking, or when he goes to the office, or when he's watching a movie? I'm talking," he said pointedly, "about *your* body."

"I take an uncommon pride in being aware, in being *concerned*, as you say, about my own body," I protested.

"It's not an uncommon pride," interjected the little man. "It's the most common sort of pride. That's why, when we're sick, and somebody (a doctor, a mother, our wife) has to be concerned with our bodies, handle them so to speak, we feel humiliated. I, on the other hand, am never—at any time—*unconcerned* about her body. Her body has a real presence (evident, I might say) in the most banal of actions: opening a door, sitting in a chair, getting on a bus."

"You help her with her body," I remarked, trying to sum it up.

"It's not a matter of protection, or compassion," protested the little man. "Quite the contrary," he said. "I find her abundance admirable. A wide body, plentiful, white, generous. Her flesh spills out, excessive, as though

23

in her case nature wanted to make a gesture of lavishness. Normal men and women (if you wish to call them 'normal') pass by unnoticed in a crowd. She, on the other hand, stands out. Hers is a body that makes us consider it, that draws our attention."

There were moments when he got excited, and I began to think that as he talked he was becoming more and more conscious of what he felt.

"Aren't you afraid of being crushed—of being overcome by the weight?" I asked ironically. "That disproportion would terrify some people," I said in an outburst of frankness.

"You might be talking about *your own* fear," he responded sagely. "I've tested that fear you're talking about with other men: they don't like the idea that she's taller, stouter, certainly stronger. They are men who are covertly domineering, even though they hide it behind good manners. They're afraid, confused. I, on the other hand, am fascinated by this disproportion. Harpooners want to defeat the whale and kill it; whereas I want to love it with its exorbitant measurements, with the awkwardness of its movements, with its courage and lack of courage," he finished.

"You want to stroll down the street with the whale," I nodded.

"She likes the fact that I'm a short, thin man," he said, not listening to my observation. "In fact, when you take a good look at it," he added, "I'm really not so short or thin: she's looking at me from her own height, from her own girth. As if we were in a fun-house filled with contorted mirrors. She thinks the disproportion of our sizes is 'amusing,'" he asserted.

"It sounds to me like you're complaining about something," I observed.

The little man looked wistful.

"I would like to do something more than simply 'amuse' her," he confessed.

"Isn't she in love with you?" I asked.

"Someone as ample, as *plentiful* as she is, can only have superficial feelings for other people."

"Do you think that just because she has such an enormous body, she's not lacking in something?" I asked, in surprise.

"There's a secret relationship between a person's body and their feelings," he acknowledged. "A body that huge has many needs, it's true: it has to eat a lot, find clothes that fit, bathe very carefully, control its metabolism with lipids and carbohydrates, but all that activity and the pleasure that goes with it, leaves little time, little possibility for loving another person. I would say that it's a matter of a body destined almost exclusively to sensuality, not to sentiments. A body that knows how to satisfy itself, that's self-sufficient."

The little man stopped, and it seemed to me that he had hit upon the place where he had doubts; perhaps it wasn't proper to go on talking.

"It's been very kind of you to listen to me," the little man thanked me, as if he had suddenly come back from a journey: the one of his cigarette smoke, the excursion to the inner terraces of fantasy. He looked at his wristwatch, and then asked me nervously: "Is it exactly six o'clock?"

I looked at my watch and answered that it was.

"Then I have to go," he said, hastily. "I have a date

25

with her at six, and it's an appointment that requires me to be right on time."

I must have given a slight sign of astonishment, or perhaps of disappointment at his leaving, because he immediately explained:

"At precisely five minutes after six, she—with a majestic step, befitting her great anatomy— will turn the corner. I, who will be plowing ahead, but from the opposite direction, will bump right smack into her. An enormous collision, do you see?" the little man said, very excited. "Only I won't crash into a wall, like a goat, but against her wide, supple bosom. I mean that I, all of me, will bump into that huge mass of flesh: my head will sink into the pillow of her breasts, they will beat my cheeks like punching bags. I'll close my eyes, jolted by the impact, and when I open them I'll see only the immense globes of her billowy breasts. My waist will hit against her belly and it, being so ample, will make me bounce back like a ball. Her large, firm arms will wrap around me then, the way a mother's wrap around her little child, and they will rock me tenderly, while she bewails the accident," he said.

And he left in a rush, without looking back at me.

I remained there, sitting in front of the window. Perhaps, if I craned my neck, I would be able to witness the encounter, the collision. A chance accident, to all appearances. I would be able to see it, but I wouldn't be able to enjoy it: I'm a tall man, well-built.

# INTIMATE DISASTERS

The bottle of bleach wouldn't open. Patricia felt frustrated, then irritated. *New top, safer,* said the label on the container. She had gone shopping on Saturday, just like she did every Saturday, at a large supermarket, well stocked with cans of beer, canned goods, pasta and laundry detergent. The bleach was the same brand as usual, and when she took it off the shelf she didn't notice the new cap. *Now, more convenient,* the label said, and to her the words seemed sarcastic. It was a quarter to seven in the morning; she had to give her son his bottle, get him dressed, put the toys and diapers in the bag, go down to the garage, start the car and hurry over to the nursery school before all the streets were jammed with traffic and made her late for work. Arteries, that's what they called the streets; with use, one or another would get clogged: they were sure to collapse.

After she dropped Andrés off at the nursery, she had fifteen minutes to cross the boulevard, drive to the office parking lot, go up the elevator, 22nd floor, Imports and Exports, Gálvez and Mautone, Inc. She had to try to get the cap open. She needed to calm down and study the instructions on the label. In fact, on the side of the bottle there was a picture, and under it some tiny letters. The picture showed the bottle cap (*New design, more convenient*), and the thin fingers of a woman, with very long fingernails). The words read: TO OPEN THIS

BOTTLE, PRESS ON THE STRIPED SECTIONS. She glanced at her wristwatch. It was almost seven o'clock. Nervously, she thought she didn't have time to look for the striped places on the bottle cap, the same way none of her lovers ever had time to search out her erogenous zones. Life was closing in: time was growing short. Even so, she was able to discover some grooves, which was the most her lovers had ever found in her. According to the instructions on the bottle, she was supposed to squeeze them with her fingers now, and unscrew the cap. One of her stupid former lovers thought it was all a matter of pressure too. She moved her hand the way the picture showed, but the cap didn't turn. NOW, LIFT THE TOP, said the instructions. When was "now"? One of her lovers had expected her to say "now" too, just before the climax. She thought that was absolutely ridiculous. The way you would teach a child to cross the street, or house-train a little dog. And yet, the marketing consultants at the company she worked for would always say that you have to treat the consumers like children: explain even the most obvious things to them. Was she a child? Did the fact that the cap wouldn't open on that damn bottle mean that the schools she had attended had failed her? Had the manufacturers of this brand of bleach designed the new cap for child-women who were raising child-sons and daughters, who in turn would beget new child-consumers until the end of days? There was a problem with the design. Or it was her. Because the cap hadn't opened. And it was getting very late. "Calm down," she thought. Being nervous will get you nowhere. Since the birth of Andrés (two years ago), her life had become rigorously programmed. She got up at six in the morning, took a

28

shower, ate her breakfast (with cereal and vitamin C), dressed (appearance was very important in a job like hers), and then she took Andrés to the daycare center. Then, from there, as fast as she possibly could, she drove to her workplace. At her job, until five o'clock in the afternoon, she turned into an independent single woman, a woman without a child, an efficient and responsible employee. The business wasn't interested in any domestic problems she might have. What's more, Patricia had the impression that a personal life did not exist for the heads of the company. Or they thought that only people who were failures had a home life.

Every time she left the office, she would go pick up Andrés. She always found him tired, half-asleep, so she drove back home at the same time that thousands and thousands of men and women in the city, who had had no home life until six in the evening, were driving back in their cars and creating huge traffic jams. Afterward, she had to feed the child, give him a bath, put him to bed and tidy up the house a little. She had very little time for personal relationships. (Under this heading, Patricia included telephone conversations with Andrés's father, or with the gynecologist who kept check on her menstrual periods and hormones. Once in a while, too, she would call someone who had once been a boyfriend or a former lover: she couldn't always remember if they had ever been one or the other, and at eleven o'clock at night, after a long, hard day at work, it really didn't matter.) On Saturdays she would go to a large supermarket and buy what she needed for the entire week. Sundays she would take Andrés to the park or to the zoo. But the city's only park was extremely dirty, and as for the zoo, the City

29

Council had put many of their animals up for sale or loan, since it was impossible to maintain them with the small budget they had. If the weather was bad, Patricia would go and visit some girlfriend who had small children too: Patricia had come to realize that women with children and women without children made up two entirely distinct types of people, separate and cut off from each other. Until she was thirty-two years old, she had belonged to the second category, but since she had brought Andrés into the world (with premeditation, let it be said), she belonged to the second type, women with children, subcategory— single mothers. In this rigorous life plan, there was no room for mistakes or improvisation. There was no room, for example, for a damn bottle cap that wouldn't open.

"Calm down," Patricia said to herself again. She could make do without the bleach, but if she did, she would feel insecure, humiliated. If she couldn't open a simple bottle of bleach, how was she going to do anything else? Before the manufacturers put the new container out on the market, they must have put it through all the proper tests. A household product in such wide use is aimed at the broad general population; manufacturers chose uncomplicated, simple designs, easily understood, within the grasp of anyone, even the most ignorant people. But she, Patricia Suárez, thirty-three years old, with a degree in Business Management, an employee of Gálvez and Mautone, Importers and Exporters, a single mother, an attractive woman, efficient and independent, was incapable of opening a bottle cap. She felt like crying. Because of the bottle cap she was running late; and besides that, she was nervous, she didn't know what clothes to wear and she was certainly going to be late to work. And she would look horrible. In her type of work, appearance was very important. *Appearance*: what a confusing concept. There was no time to become familiar with anything or anyone; you had to let yourself be led by appearances, it was all a question of image. She was going to tell her psychoanalyst about the incident with the bottle cap. When you don't have a good lover, you need a good psychoanalyst: just like you need a good lawyer or a good dentist. For matters of hygiene, like a facial scrub, washing your hair, or clearing out your mind. She had been seeing a psychoanalyst even before Andrés was born. In fact, she had held a discussion with herself, in the presence of the impartial or indifferent (Patricia didn't know which) ear of the psychoanalyst, about whether or not to have a baby. "Whatever you decide," he had said, "you have my support." Patricia thought she would have liked a man—not the psychoanalyst—to have said the same thing. But there hadn't been one. Andrés's father had not wanted to have children, and when he found out that Patricia was pregnant, he thought he had been duped. So he agreed—grudgingly—to have his paternity limited to his name on the child's record, at the Registry Office. He didn't want children, and Patricia didn't want a husband: sometimes it's easier to know what one doesn't want. As she was trying to open the bottle cap, Patricia thought that the most stable relationship she had had in her life was with the psychoanalyst. It occurred to her that a male psychoanalyst is like a billy goat: he likes to have a herd of dependent, submissive, frustrated females who will work for him and who will consult him about everything, as if he were the great male, the Alpha male, the patriarch, the supreme authority, God. If she told the psychoanalyst about the stubborn cap on the bleach bottle, he would undoubtedly ask her to analyze the possible meanings of the word "cap." She would say that when she looked at a bottle top (especially if it was the cork in a bottle of wine or champagne), she thought of Antonio, Andrés's father, because he was so squat-looking. Then she would immediately add that she had always liked ugly men, maybe because she felt more secure with them: at least she was more attractive.

The bottle of bleach wouldn't open. It was seven-thirty, she still hadn't woken Andrés and she hadn't decided what clothes to wear. It crossed her mind that she could go out to the landing and, with the bottle of bleach in her hand, knock on a neighbor's door and ask him to open it. At that early hour, most of the men in the building would be shaving, getting ready for work, and although the rhythms of modern life hinder neighbors who live on the same floor from meeting and doing one another small favors, like lending a little flour, a cup of milk or a corkscrew, the vision of a weak, defenseless woman, flummoxed by a container with an impossible lid, would appeal to the vanity of any male in the world. The neighbor, wearing his pajama bottoms and with shaving cream covering half his face, would come to the door, and with one motion, firm, smart, virile (like the blade of a sword) would deflower the bottle, would cut its throat. He would hand the deflowered bottle back to her with a smug smile on his lips and utter some gallant phrase like: "It only needed a little muscle," or "Call me any time you have a problem": an ambiguous and self-satisfied phrase that would reinforce his masculine superiority. She would accept it humbly, because it was so late and because her mother had always told her how difficult it was for a woman to live alone, without a man at her side.

After she had heard her so many times (her mother had been left a widow when she was very young), Patricia had the feeling that this difficulty (the one that her mother drummed on repeatedly) was a confusing mixture of broken electric plugs, sticking doors, household repairs, being afraid at night, loneliness and helplessness. She felt like the difficulty had some obscure relationship to the bottle cap. With no man around to fix the electric plugs and open rebellious bottle tops, Patricia had considered the possibility of hiring a housekeeper. But she didn't make enough even to pay for the rent on the apartment, the child-care, her gasoline, suitable clothing for her work—which was very exacting, the beauty salon, and her weekly session with the psychoanalyst. The psychoanalyst was much more expensive than a housekeeper, although in both cases it was a matter of cleaning. The psychoanalyst was not only the Alpha-male of the herd: he was also a chimney sweep. Then, while she was struggling with the bottle cap, she remembered that she had a business lunch-date with the director of a company that made women's lingerie. Women's lingerie had become fashionable in recent years, and instead of simple, unadorned coitus, many people preferred to find enjoyment with a line of garters, panties, brassieres, and harnesses that fired the imagination. She couldn't waste any more time. She had to wake Andrés, bathe him, give him his bottle and dress him. She looked hostilely at the bottle of bleach, pristine, in its yellow container and with its blue cap, as it stood straight, unbowed, despite all her efforts. No, it wasn't because she lacked the ability: there had to be a mistake in the way it was manufactured. Whoever designed the lid must have been a man. A conceited, smug male, all full of himself. He designed a worthless bottle top, a top that the hands of a woman could not open, because he, in all likelihood, had never looked closely at a woman's hands, at how slight, how delicate they were. This new contraption had replaced the old one and now, at this very moment, in Barcelona, in New York, in Los Angeles and in Buenos Aires (this bleach was an important, multinational brand), thousands of women were struggling, trying to unscrew the cap, while Andrés was starting to cry, he must have woken up hungry and anxious, his biological clock had urgent demands, it was telling him that something was not going right, there had been an accident, a breakdown, mama-the giver, mama-the good breast, was not coming to feed him, was not cradling him, was not kissing him, was not washing him, was not dressing him. Andrés was starting to cry just like she was on the verge of crying. It was getting late, the child was hungry, she was behind schedule and the boss didn't accept any excuses, like all bosses he had no personal life, and as a result he didn't have any bleach or any bottle caps; her boss was an arrogant type who had no clothes that needed to be washed, no suits that had to be cleaned; after he had worn a pair of socks, he threw them in the trash, he ate out at restaurants and he had no children. In the morning Andrés only drank milk if it was given to him in a baby bottle. It was apparently a holdover from the time he was not yet weaned. When we wake up, thought Patricia, nearly all of us are babies. We demand a bottle, not a cup; we want honey with our cereal, not sugar. That's the way it was: children are riddled with desire, something that adults are not able to allow themselves. Did the bottle of bleach have a desire to remain closed? "Don't be a fool," Patricia told herself, "objects don't have desires." All right then, if it wasn't the bottle's desire, it must have been the desire of the person who invented the cap. No woman would ever have dreamed of having to force open a bottle of bleach. To be honest, the inventor had designed the perfect cap: mute and still in its oppression, incapable of being opened, of spilling out its treasure, like some keratinous virginities. (She couldn't remember where she had read that. It must have been in some magazine at the dentist's office or at the hair salon. Those were the only places where she had time to read.) The inventor had to be the sort of person who didn't like things to overflow; he thought things always had to be kept contained. Trapped. Possibly, for him, the bottle of bleach was a phallic symbol. Preserve the semen, don't squander it or waste it, don't throw it away uselessly.

Like Antonio who always made love wearing a condom so that he wouldn't father a child. Still, she could have sworn that Antonio looked at the seminal fluid with nostalgia as he flushed it down the toilet; maybe he was sorry that it had to be wasted. Semen always smelled a little like bleach. And Andrés was crying. Patricia was going to make a decision: she would abandon the bottle of bleach with its airtight, indestructible cap. She would leave it, flaunting its impenetrable virginity, on the table, and she would forget the incident. The last time she had cried over anything like this was when the plumbing got stopped up. No one had ever taught her how plumbing works: not in high school, not at Business School. And the plumbing in the building where she lived got clogged up

35

when she was away, insidiously, while she was at the office. She had come back home innocently, the way she did every day, not knowing that when she turned on the water the pipes were going to burst. Without warning. Suddenly, from the bowels of the building some strange, foul-smelling, bubbling, gross-colored slime began to come out. She couldn't understand what was happening. She had rented the apartment recently, and for a rate that could by no means be considered a bargain. And now, suddenly, it seemed like the apartment was coming apart at the seams, that it was liquefying into repugnant matter, like that painting, *Europe After the Rain*, that she had seen at an exhibition. She tried using the telephone to get help, but the voice of an answering machine told her that because of a problem with the lines in that area, we deeply regret to inform you that the telephone service is not operating at this time. And the water continued to make its way over the floors. She burst into tears, not knowing what to do. Then, even though he was completely unexpected, Antonio, the father of her little boy, appeared. He was always appearing and disappearing without warning, it was a type of control, but she had never said anything to him. "Not everything can be said," observed the psychoanalyst on one occasion, but Patricia thought that with Antonio nothing could be said. He was very touchy. Antonio opened the door with his own key (that he never wanted to give back to her: he insisted that he ought to have a key to the house where his son was living) and saw her in the middle of the living room, crying, while dark, sticky water oozed over the floor, threatening to get his shoes wet. He was a very dapper man, highly obsessed with his clothing, and could not help making a grimace of disgust. His expression only caused Patricia's sobbing to increase. In fact, she couldn't care less if Antonio got his shoes and the cuff of his pants dirty, but she felt inexplicably guilty and insecure, she was filled with self-pity and she continued to cry. He didn't say a word (with one observant and thorough glance he took in the entire situation: the clogged pipes, the flooded floor, Patricia's crying, her guilt and helplessness), and after studying the scene, he quickly walked to the kitchen, to a panel hidden between the baseboard and the wall, inside a box, and with a couple of energetic turns, decidedly masculine, he cut off the flow of water. Surprised, Patricia stopped crying. The worker who put in the plumbing, when she moved into the flat, had told her not to touch those valves no matter what, and she had followed his orders so judiciously that she had completely forgotten about them.

As soon as the water stopped pouring out, Antonio called the super on the building's intercom (which was working now), and paid him to mop up the water that was flooding the apartment. Men were so efficient that way. Self-satisfied, he felt generous, and he invited her, along with the child, to have a drink at the bar on the corner, while the super was mopping up the floor. They didn't talk about anything, but he gave her a piece of advice. He told her: "You shouldn't cry just because of a broken pipe." Then Patricia, very calmly and very serenely, threw the contents of the drink in his face, the liquid, complete with its tiny orange bubbles. The liquid splashed on the lapel of his new clean-cut suit that he was wearing for the first time.

Now she was crying again, but there was no one she could throw the bottle of bleach at. Sniffling, she began to dress the child.

"Don't think I'm crying just because the lid on the bottle of bleach wouldn't open," she explained to him, in a sort of soliloquy. "That's not why; it's because it started to make me suspect something. It's true that at first I thought there was something wrong with me. I thought it was my fault, that I just couldn't do it. But it's not me, it's the bottle cap. They've made a new container, and it's defective, and they've put those bottles out on the shelves, and innocently, we've bought them. It's their fault that I'm running late, and we're going to be late for the nursery and for work. I won't be able to tell my boss something as simple as that the cap on the bottle of bleach wouldn't open. He's a very professional man, very important: he has no home life. The only things that concern him are stock prices, marketing wars, currency speculation, and advertising campaigns. The most I can say is that I was late because I got stuck in traffic. Traffic jams, my boy, are very respectable. They are more respectable than a headache, the illness of a relative or broken plumbing. And you," she continued, addressing the child but as though talking to herself, "didn't cry just because you were hungry. You cried because the cap on the bleach bottle wouldn't open, because I was nervous and had doubts about myself."

That afternoon, while she was driving to the psychoanalyst's office (everything had gone relatively well, despite the delay), she thought women's tears, spread throughout the city, were a white river, burning, a river of lava, a river beyond imagination, running through its dark bowels, a nameless river that appeared on no maps.

"The cap on the bleach wouldn't open," Patricia

38

told the psychoanalyst as soon as the session began, "and I'm in no mood to waste my time on any interpretations. It's a fact: the new cap they made for that brand doesn't work. I called the product's distributor. They've gotten a lot of complaints. The new cap was designed by an industrial engineer, burning for success, I suppose, strong, sure of himself, but he was a failure. They're going to take the bottles out of circulation. As for myself," Patricia asserted decisively, "I'm going to put in a claim for compensation."

"To the product manufacturer?" asked the psychoanalyst in surprise.

"To Andrés's father, of course," answered Patricia. "He doesn't take care of any expenses. It's like the child doesn't concern him."

When she got home, Patricia went straight to the kitchen. She took out a knife with a sharp point, and without hesitation she stuck a hole through the cap. She stabbed it right down the center with a clean, perfect cut. The bottle lost all its virility.

# THE WITNESS

I grew up among my mother's lady-friends. I don't know how many there were, I can't even say I remember them all, but some of them I haven't forgotten. And even though I may not have seen them again, or if they only show up at our house once in a while, I know who they are, and I have fond memories of them. I never played with other children, just with my mother's friends. In fact, I'm a very solitary sort, I prefer computer games to the company of others like me. Computer games, or my mother's lady-friends. In the first place, they show up one at a time. There are whole stretches of time when my mother has only one friend, and that one practically lives at our house, she eats with us, we watch TV programs and videos together, she takes walks with us, plays games, spends the night. They have always been very nice to me.

"I really like it that there aren't other men in our house," I told my mother, grateful to her for the fact that my childhood wasn't tormented by the deafening shouting of a violent father or a demanding lover.

Women are much sweeter. I get along with them better. I wouldn't have liked sharing my house with other men; but I found it lovely to share it with my mother's friends.

I think my mother felt the same way. From the time she and my father separated—when I was very small—the only visitors that came to the house were women, and that was very comforting. I suppose it was for my father too. The first one that I can remember was a girl with very dark skin, a high pitched voice, and dazzling black eyes. My mother was very young then, and I was only three years old. We went on lots of walks together; I slept in my bedroom, and the two of them, together, in my mother's room. But sometimes I got up at night, and went into the big bedroom. Then, one of them would take me in her arms and cradle me, and I would fall asleep between them, cuddled in the warmth of their naked bodies. Then there was another one who had long blond hair, and it felt so good to let my fingers disappear into it, like summer butterflies. My mother combed it very carefully while I watched, gliding the wide tortoiseshell comb through that silky hair that reached nearly down to her waist. (At the time and many other times, I was sorry that I hadn't been born a girl so that my mother would comb my hair with all that devotion and care; and there were many times when I regretted being a boy with short hair and, because of that, missing out on something that gave them so much pleasure.) There was another one, however, with a more masculine appearance: she had broad shoulders, was thickset, her voice was very deep, and she seemed to be a very strong woman. She was always buying me a lot of toys: she gave me a bicycle, a bunch of puzzles, she was always asking me to play games competing against her, she would challenge me at jumping, boxing, swimming. I didn't care for her as much as I did the others, but I really liked the way she was always clowning around, and I enjoyed beating her at chess. My mother was a little annoyed at all the attention she gave me, and I think they argued about it once or twice, but I calmed my mother down by telling her that, beyond any shadow of a doubt, I liked her best, and that she was more beautiful and more intelligent.

The last one was a young actress. She had starred in a movie that I didn't see, because my mother didn't think it was appropriate for me. We had to protect her, that's what my mother told me. She'd had a hard childhood, and now she needed to learn a lot of things before she got on with her career: we were going to give her a home and teach her all the things she needed to know.

My mother is a very generous woman. She's always helping someone, and she brought me up to be the same way. We've helped a lot of women, although they've disappeared from our house afterward. They find a roof, their meals, warmth, music and tenderness in our home. You could see from a distance that what the young actress needed was protection: although she was happy, amusing and very nice, she wasn't a very steady person, and she was terribly disorganized.

"You will learn how to study with my son," my mother told her.

In fact, from the very beginning my mother gave her things to do: she told her to practice English, French, and she gave her a list of books to read from the library in our house.

It was beautiful to see them reading old poets together, listening to opera, and trying on clothes, wearing each other's outfits. Sometimes the actress would put on a skirt and blouse that belonged to my mother; other times, it was my mother who would wear her pants, the English hat and white scarf. I knew, from talking to my mother, that the actress had run away from home, that it really wasn't a home, and now she had finally found one in our house.

"Her company will do you good," my mother told me, "you've been keeping to yourself more and more everyday."

I liked her company, in fact. Helena had big, blue eyes, she was tall and thin, and her neck, so very long and white, was like the neck of a glass. I was enthralled by her. I let her come into my room—even my mother didn't have my permission to go there—, I showed her my drawings, she listened to my favorite records. I liked looking at her. Her movements were fluid and subtle, not clumsy like mine (I've grown a lot lately, and my arms and legs aren't always the most graceful); her voice had a delicate, soft tone, but it was very suggestive, and when she got close to me I felt vague, shivering sensations. I especially liked looking at my Lepidoptera collection with her. She was awed by the patterns on the butterflies' wings, and she quickly learned to classify them. We took several trips out to the countryside, looking for rare species, while my mother waited for us in the car, reading one of her books.

My mother taught her how to cook too, and sometimes she surprised us, making a dish for us that we liked.

At night they slept together in my mother's bedroom. I tried to put off that moment, because I'd gotten so used to their company that I had no desire to go to bed. But once my mother ordered me to go, it was very hard to make her change her mind.

In the morning, before I went to school, I would go to my mother's bedroom to say goodbye. The door was

43

always closed; I would tap on it softly, and when I knew that my mother was awake, I would push it a little and go into the darkened room. It was somewhat difficult for me to see them in the dim light, but after a while my eyes made out two bodies, one next to the other. Helena was always asleep: she must have been a very sound sleeper. Then, without making any noise, I would kiss my mother and say goodbye. But one time I went in without knocking and I found Helena half-asleep, wearing a see-through gown; her fresh, budding breasts were visible under the cloth, and her firm, lustrous thighs appeared between the sheets.

I was electrified at the sight. At school that day I couldn't concentrate, I was distracted, restless, and this really surprised my teachers.

I went back home, nervous and excited, hoping to find Helena. She was just there, in the kitchen, making dessert, and I contented myself with cornering her, jumping and bounding around her to get her attention.

"Be still," she told me, laughing.

I adored her laughter. It was playful, daring, a little bit childish. My mother's laughter, on the other hand, was deep, low, mature. The laughter of a woman who knows how to be severe.

After dinner, the two of them stayed in the parlor, reading a book together. I walked around in my room nervously, without any desire to study or to play with my computer. I wanted to be with Helena, but it was the time of day when she belonged to my mother.

I went into the bathroom and masturbated. I did it while thinking of Helena's breasts and my mother's legs. Ah, my mother's legs. Before, when I was little, my mother used to walk around the house almost naked, displaying her beautiful white legs. They are broad, lustrous, like two Roman columns. I didn't find even Helena's legs as appealing as my mother's. Now, ever since Helena has been with us, my mother has stopped walking around nearly naked in front of me.

After a while I heard the door to the big bedroom close. The two of them must have gone to lie down on the bed for a while, together. To imagine what was happening then, gave me both pain and pleasure at the same time. I could picture, as though on a screen, my mother removing her white, silk blouse, and Helena taking off her black, velvet pants. I could picture my mother's skin, and Helena's white skin. I could see them comparing their breasts, their thighs, their pubes. All in silence, so they would not arouse my curiosity. All in silence, so that they could pretend they were sleeping.

I didn't need to spy on them through the keyhole. I knew that scene, even though I had never witnessed it. The door was still blocked, with the two of them inside, closed off to me. I was the one who was excluded, cast out, gone. I dreamed up a thousand subterfuges so I could barge in, interrupt the scene taking place inside my mother's bedroom, but I knew that in the end I wouldn't use any of them, I was such a coward. I didn't have the courage to interrupt my mother, I wasn't sure, either, if I could resist the vision of the two symmetrical bodies, sprawled out on the bed.

That evening, at dinner, I had no appetite, and I was rather hostile. I finally made my mother mad, and she cried out:

"I'd like to know what's going on with you.

45

You're in a horrible mood."

But Helena stuck up for me. She winked at me and smiled, and she touched my leg under the table. Her complicity made me feel better. I held her foot a little with my own, and I deliberately tipped a glass a wine over on the tablecloth just to irritate my mother.

That night I went to my room, listening to them argue in the parlor. My little rash of bad temper had been able to upset them. And content with this small bit of revenge, I closed the door to my room.

A week later I won the Drawing Award in a contest they held at my school. I came home, very excited, all set to make my mother very happy. I used my key to open the door, and I couldn't find anybody at home. It's true that I had gotten back earlier than expected, but I was thrilled about the award and I wanted to show it to her. The house was completely silent. I was going to go into my bedroom when I noticed a light coming from my mother's room. I went up to the door—it was closed—and I knocked.

"I have a headache," answered my mother, not opening the door.

But I heard movements going on in the room, a rustling of clothes and sheets.

I sensed that Helena was inside. I had an anxiety attack, my eyes filled with tears.

"I'll be there in a minute," my mother announced, noticing, perhaps, that I hadn't gone away from the door.

But I barged into the bedroom. I think I blushed. My mother was half dressed, crouched down on the floor like a dog, looking around for the rest of her clothes. It aggravated me to find her in that position.

"Get out of here!" she demanded imperiously, but I didn't move.

Her feet were bare, and she was wearing only a lacy, black leotard. I saw her beautiful white legs, her full breasts barely concealed by the mesh, her ardent lips, her mussed hair. At her side, still stretched out on the bed, was Helena. She burst out laughing, stupidly. She was naked, and when she saw me she tried to cover herself with the sheet.

I threw myself on both of them. I'm very tall, and with all my strength I forced my mother onto the bed. In surprise, she let out a deep, furious shout:

"Get out!"

I managed to hold them both down on the bed. Helena was laughing foolishly, nervously. My mother, on the other hand, was astonished, and couldn't understand what had made me burst into the room, breaking the tacit agreement between us. I held them both down with my arms, and I gave a deep wail too, deafening, painful.

Now Helena had begun to cry. I don't like women who cry. I never saw my mother cry: I don't think she ever let herself show any weakness like that in front of me. Suddenly I despised Helena for being such a baby.

"Kiss her!" I ordered.

Helena sat up on the bed, covering herself with the sheet while I held my mother down, and looked at me in surprise, tears streaming down her face.

Suddenly, I pulled the sheets from the bed. It was with a quick, violent motion. Helena's body appeared, long and slender, the accentuated bones of her shoulders, her nipples like purple grapes, the very dark down of her pubis, her red toenails. I saw my mother's broad neck too,

47

still with pink patches, her milky white arms.

"Kiss her!" I commanded.

Sobbing, Helena bent timidly over my mother. She kissed her on the mouth. It was a clumsy, awkward kiss, but I insisted:

"Kiss her!"

My mother struggled to pull away from my arms, but she is not a very strong woman despite being so tall, and she wasn't able to free herself.

"Now," I ordered, "hold her breasts."

Helena looked at me, doubtfully.

"Do it!" I roared.

I saw that she was afraid of me. Slowly, hesitantly, Helena moved her hands closer to my mother's breasts.

"You're crazy," she screamed, trying to get away from me.

"You got away once," I retorted. "But this time you won't be able to," I added.

Helena's trembling hands enveloped my mother's breasts.

"Her nipples," I indicated. "Squeeze her nipples."

Helena looked at me, her eyes full of fear.

"Do it," I urged her.

Helena touched her fleetingly.

"More," I said.

Now her fingers squeezed my mother's nipples tightly.

"That's it," I said, nodding my head.

"Get on top of her," I added.

"What?" murmured Helena in astonishment.

"I said get on her!" I shouted.

With one quick motion I had my mother sprawled

out on the bed. I liked seeing her like that, lying down half naked, with the black nylon and lace leotard barely covering her belly, her waist, the lower part of her breasts. In her groin some dark, curly hairs of the pubis peeked out.

Helena very gently lay down on her.

"That's it," I murmured.

Her body, more lithe and firm, covered my mother's. I gazed at Helena's shorter hair, her round buttocks, her bare feet. My mother's body was barely visible under Helena's. Her arms rested on the pillow, and their foreheads touched. Now I saw four breasts, four legs, two bodies united, like a marvelous double statue, like two Siamese twin sisters joined by the umbilical cord.

Then I quickly took off my pants and I climbed onto the back of the pyramid that their bodies made.

On top, I was the third figure of the triptych, the only one who was moving convulsively. I set myself firmly on their thighs, and pressed the two bodies under my weight. I quickly penetrated Helena from behind. She cried out. My mother, underneath, sprawled out on the bed, was panting.

I exploded like a flower torn asunder. I burst into flame. Then, exhausted, I withdrew. I left them quickly. Before closing the door, I said to my mother:

"Don't worry about me. I'm every bit a man now. The one that was missing from this house."

# THE MOST WONDERFUL
# WEEK OF OUR LIVES

We were in a hotel suite on Lexington Avenue, in New York. Eva had booked the suite; I wouldn't have had the nerve. The suite had two levels: the Jacuzzi, the stereo and the refrigerator were on the lower, on the upper level there was an enormous double bed, with several sets of lights, a bar and a video screen, for erotic films I supposed. There was also a writing desk, complete with its computer and fax machine, because anyone who had a glamorous erotic life must have important public or private business too.

We had taken the suite the night before, I think, because after making love standing up, in bed, from the rear, on the carpet, against the refrigerator, she on top, I on the bottom, naked or wearing the erotic lingerie we had bought at a sex-shop on 45th Street, my sense of time was as weak and feeble as my energy. We didn't make love all through the night: occasionally we stopped to drink some very cold champagne that Eva took from the refrigerator, or to eat those marvelous tropical fruits, with deep colors and a uniform taste—like plastic—that are so abundant in the grocery stores of New York. It was precisely during one of those pauses (while I was investigating the multiple erotic possibilities of peanuts that you're always able to find in hotel refrigerators and on the trays in airplanes) that Eva said:

"I have to call my husband on the phone. Do you

mind if I do it from the bedroom?"

The question hit me like a bucket of cold water. Something that I definitely needed, thanks to our amatory exercises. I stretched out a hand toward the night table, not realizing that the bed was so large that my arm couldn't reach it: my hand made a ridiculous pirouette in the air, the same way I was feeling. Fortunately, Eva wasn't looking at me right at that moment, so I pulled myself together, took up a pack of Peter Stuyvesants with dignity, and gaining time, I slowly lit a cigarette.

"You didn't tell me you were married," I observed in a husky voice.

My hoarseness was due to the excesses of love as much as it was to the jolt I had felt.

"You didn't ask me," Eva replied defensively, drawing her white bathrobe together.

I've observed that women who wear white bathrobes are accustomed to fastening them resolutely at certain moments. It's when they've decided to become serious or to end a love-making session. Like when the doors of the theater are closed after the play has ended, chasing out the last spectators, the ones who would like to ask for an autograph, prolong the work, or have a cup of coffee with the actors in the nearest bar. That gesture of women who wear a bathrobe means, more or less: "My dear boy/girl: The shop—her body—is closed for today. The love-making is over. Now I am a woman who is dressed, that is, I am my own master. Everything that's happened between us (men /women) is part of the past; it was very nice, but it's over. If you want it to go on for another day, we'll have to negotiate the conditions." Dressed in her bathrobe, Eva became inaccessible at the

51

very moment that she was confessing she had a husband.

"I'm not used to asking people about their marital status," I replied. "It's something that honesty and openness require us to tell, without needing to ask questions."

Eva had sat down on the sofa in the room, far from the bed. Despite the fact that the strap on her bathrobe was pulled tightly around her, her beautiful golden legs were exposed, flung out to either side, with the precision and elegance of a drafting compass, plus a certain lassitude—unquestionably lustful, that aroused obscene desires in me.

"If I had told you I was married, you wouldn't have gone to bed with me," she asserted.

Precisely. I have two principles in my life. The first is: "Do unto others as you would have them do unto you," and the second is: "Married women have an owner. They are private property. Steer clear of them if you want to avoid problems."

"I wouldn't have gone to bed with you," I lied, feeling out of sorts. "I don't care for married women," I continued. "They wear a ring on their finger, they're never satisfied, and they mix love up with money."

"Those are prejudices," Eva protested. "Give me a cigarette," she ordered.

"You don't smoke," I reproached her while I took a Peter Stuyvesant from the pack and held it out to her.

If she had known me better she would have known that I only offer someone an unlit cigarette when I'm really angry.

"And you don't go to bed with married women," Eva replied.

I had the feeling that we were going to get into an

52

argument. I'm very good at arguing when I'm dressed, standing up, or at a table in a café; but right after making love, I'm absolutely useless, incapable of thinking.

"I feel cheated on," I declared.

I made an effort to stand up. Betrayed, and in bed, I felt extremely vulnerable. People who are hunted down by the police, sleep in their clothes; I'd seen it in the movies, and a friend of mine who was a guerrilla had told me so.

"I wasn't trying to cheat on you," answered Eva. "I wanted to go to bed with you, I couldn't bear having any obstacle in the way."

Even though it seemed to me like a lovely confession, and one that was worthy of absolute forgiveness, I decided not to back down.

"There is one," I replied severely.

"No, there isn't," she disagreed. "Since yesterday evening you've proved that there isn't any."

"All right," I said. "Yesterday, Friday, I began to make love with a single woman, and today, Saturday, I woke up making love to a woman who is married."

"As far as that goes," Eva countered, "I think you're married too. For the first two hours after we met, you never stopped talking about your friend, Lucía."

"That was a defense mechanism," I confessed. "I thought that if I kept talking about her, I might be able to resist wanting you." My strategy had failed completely. "Besides, Lucía is not my wife, or my girlfriend, or anything like that," I answered indignantly. "I'm not her wife either. Our names aren't together on any written documents, we don't receive marital benefits, we don't have children, we don't celebrate a wedding anniversary,

53

nobody gives us an electric toaster for Christmas. If one of us dies, the other won't receive a widow's pension. The fact that there's no word that's given to this sort of relationship is proof of its authenticity. Lucía and I are *friends*."

"Do you go to bed with all your lady friends?" she asked me, playing the innocent.

"We're going to have an argument about lovers," I thought to myself. Sometimes love is so strong, so unbearable, so overwhelming that lovers need a good fight to become autonomous, painfully independent, masters of themselves again. It's that way with homosexuals, and with heterosexuals too.

"I only go to bed with my girlfriends if they're pretty and not married."

"What about the divorced ones?" Eva asked ironically. "Do you go to bed with divorced women, or are they out of bounds too, like the married ones?"

I felt a shiver of dread run through me. It was caused by the word "divorced." The other part of my second principle ("Married women have an owner. Steer clear of them.") says the following: "Married women, besides the fact that they're married, have the drawback that the first time they go to bed with a woman, they immediately want to divorce their husband and marry the woman."

"I'm not interested in divorcees," I declared. "They're usually addicted to marriage; they're hoping for a second chance, and it makes no difference whether it's with a man, a woman, a dog or a cat."

"I don't think I'm the first married woman who's ever been in your life," murmured Eva suspiciously.

I was in no mood for making confessions. In any case, not open confessions.

"My first *girlfriend* was married. She got a divorce, and we lived together for three years. A bona fide idyll."

"What happened after that?" asked Eva.

In the manuals, they call this tactic "dissuasion."

"Don't you know that three years, three months and three days is the precise amount of time that passion lasts? Everything else," I added ironically, "is marriage."

"You resent married women," Eva insisted.

"I don't resent married women," I said emphatically. "We're different species. Like men and women," I added. "I never have anything to talk about, with married women," I explained. "Married women inevitably end up talking about their husband's gastritis, or the problems their children are having in school, or their frigidity, or the mortgage on their house."

"I've not said one word to you about my husband," Eva countered. "And besides, I don't have any children."

"But now you have to call him on the phone," I answered.

"It's for *our own* peace and quiet, my dear," she explained cryptically. "A brief telephone call, and we won't have to worry about a thing, all the rest of the time."

And this is how a husband watches out for his wife's happiness. Or to put it another way, I was beginning to be indebted to a husband.

"Thank you, my dear," I said in the most insincere tone of voice I could muster. "I won't have a care in the world, now that I know your husband is protecting us."

It was a low blow, I know. But she deserved it

because of her initial lie ("Omission," as she would put it).

"I'm going to take a shower," I announced. "The telephone is all yours."

I don't like New York. I don't like the smell of cooking oil you get out on the streets, or the traffic jams on Fifth Avenue, or the beggars in Central Park, or the unintelligible English they jabber, or the manholes that belch out steam. The city strikes me as dirty and uninviting. I had arrived there a week earlier to take part in a translators' conference that I hadn't been able to get out of. Eva was the representative of some international organization—the sort that puts together endless banquets to deal with world hunger, but, unlike me, she lived in New York. We met, by chance, at a queer bar in the Village, the only area of the city where I don't feel uncomfortable. I'd gone to the bar to have a drink, smoke a joint and glance over the New York fauna, lesbian women section. It was impossible not to see Eva, in spite of the fact that the bar was packed and that smoke was hanging over the counter, the tables and the pool tables. It was impossible not to see her for the simple reason that she stood out from all the other women, not just because of her height, but because of her desire to exhibit herself. She had luxuriant, flowing locks of red hair, thick lips, firm hips, and a tone of voice that she could inflect in various registers, like an experienced actress. She danced alone on one of the dance floors, conscious that everyone was watching her, checking her out. When the loud band launched into a reggae number, Eva left the dance floor and walked over to the bar where I was, admiring her and drinking a whiskey. Then we recognized each other. In fact, that very morning we had seen each other in the main hall of the hotel where they were holding an international conference and one of those boring sessions of the translators' convention. Among the tables filled with cups of steaming coffee, sandwiches, orange and tomato juice, we conference members wasted our time miserably, although they were paying us for it.

There usually aren't any married women in lesbian bars, and if there are, they're divorcees. When we complicitly recognized each other, I was the victim of a reasonable deduction, I told myself as I finished drying off in the luxurious bathtub in the hotel suite on Lexington Avenue: I thought she was a single woman. Eva was still on the phone, talking to her husband. From the walk-in closet in the bathroom I heard a few "honeys" and "loves" that drove me up the wall, no doubt because of my disgust with the English language. I thought she had to be married to some wholesome, conventional Yankee. The sort that eats non-fat yogurt, that doesn't drink wine, doesn't smoke, and keeps their cholesterol in check in hopes that they'll live to be two-hundred years old. So on some evenings Eva, his wife, would escape to a women's bar, looking for intense emotions. And she found them: she certainly found them. I was the proof. While talking to her husband, Eva used a false, high-pitched voice, as though she were a soprano. If she had used that on me, I wouldn't be taking a shower in the luxurious tub at a hotel on Lexington Avenue. She was faking it. Or was she faking it when she talked to me?

When I came back into the room, Eva had an innocent, satisfied look on her face, like Little Miss Goody Two-Shoes.

"That's done," she told me.

"What's done?" I asked, pretending to be dumb.

"I talked to my husband. Now we can do whatever we want to."

I had no doubts about what we wanted to do, and it seemed to me that from the moment we met at the bar two days before, we had done only what we wanted to do. Even so, I said:

"Did he give us his permission?"

Eva ignored the cutting remark.

"I told him that the committee's work was going to take another week."

"And he believed you?" I asked skeptically.

"Of course," asserted Eva, as if no one could doubt her honesty.

"Did you give him the name of the hotel and the room's telephone number?" I asked, taken aback.

"He didn't ask me for them," Eva said.

"I didn't ask you if you were married, either," I reminded her.

"I don't usually give out information that people don't ask me for," Eva declared.

"I suppose you call that *privacy*," I said ironically.

"I call it being cautious," she answered. "Did you give the telephone number of the hotel to your girlfriend?" she countered.

"I'm away on a trip," I said in self defense. "On another continent."

"And with even more reason," she said accusingly. "My husband is only in New Jersey, just a few miles from here. You're much further away."

"I usually call my girlfriend," I said, "but I try to be alone in the room."

"Something that must not happen to you very often," she scoffed.

That put an end to the subject of marriage.

She kissed me on the mouth, toyed with the rebellious bangs that fall down over my forehead, and said:

"We have a whole week just to ourselves alone. I hope it will be the most wonderful week of our lives."

The most wonderful week of our lives flew by very quickly. When all is said and done, it was only seven days, no matter how you look at it. Even the most wonderful week of our lives has a Sunday that comes on the heels of a Saturday, and then, in a flash, the other weeks begin, the ones that aren't wonderful but that last much longer.

The other feature of the most wonderful week of our lives is that Monday, Tuesday, Wednesday, Thursday, Friday, Saturday and Sunday are taken up with the same thing, making love, so that when the most wonderful week of our lives is over, several pounds of weight have been lost, enormous bags under the eyes have been gained, there is a trembling in the body's extremities that resembles early onset Parkinson's, and none of the questions that you wanted to ask (what is your favorite movie?, how do you vote?, how much money do you make?, are your parents still alive?, what writers do you like?) have been asked, except for one: do you love me? We didn't even know if we'd been tested for AIDS.

I had to go to Washington because of my work, and Eva needed to go back home because of her marriage. We figured that I could be back in New York in a week, and we reserved the same suite in the same hotel: we were beginning to be fetishists, which is what commonly happens to people when they fall in love.

Washington is one of the most boring cities in the world, or at least that's the way I felt, so I took advantage of my free time after the workshops, and got caught up on my sleep: the most wonderful week of our lives had used up almost all my energy. I lost my self-control only once, and dialed Eva's telephone number in New Jersey: the husband answered and I hung up. I also called Lucía. I explained to her that the conference had been extended, that I was sick and tired of traveling by air, that I didn't like American food, and that I went to bed early to watch videos of my favorite singers on the TV at the hotel.

When I got back to New York, Frank was waiting for me at the airport. Frank was Eva's husband. "Courtesy of the house," he said, putting my suitcase into his car like a perfect gentleman. They had arranged, he said, "to give me an intimate lunch. To welcome me back." "That's just like a marriage," I thought. "A madhouse with no doors or windows, where even the telephone is tapped." It wasn't just mad men and mad women who got married. People who weren't crazy before they got married, were stricken soon afterward. I looked despondently at my navy blue suitcase as it was swallowed up by the gigantic mouth of Frank's Plymouth: neither my suitcase nor I knew what our destiny would be.

Frank had prepared a light lunch, full of those horrible American sauces named after movie actors or actresses. And that wasn't the worst. The worst part, without a doubt, was having to swallow the Paul Newman hamburgers and the Elizabeth Taylor potatoes, while sitting on a wicker chair across from Eva who was eating with an astonishing appetite, and beside Frank who insisted on talking to me about the next war in Europe. Frank was convinced that the resurgence of nationalism on the Old Continent was putting the Western World in peril. The United States would have to intervene, again, to save what was left of the European democracies. I had no interest in having Frank save me from anything, but I was willing, willing and ready, to save Eva from the perils of a boring marriage, a stodgy husband and a frustrating menopause. At coffee-time— and *only at coffee-time*—did I have a chance to be alone with Eva for a few minutes in the kitchen, and I said to her:

"Whose brilliant idea was it to have this American lunch?"

"Dear," she answered, "it's just this once. So that Frank can meet you and so he won't be jealous. He thinks you're simply wonderful," she informed me.

"I think his wife is much more so," I murmured.

"He'll be gone soon, and we'll have all the time to ourselves," said Eva.

"I don't have any desire to wait. No desire, and no reason to," I declared brazenly.

"Do it for me. It won't be long, and besides, Frank will adore you. He's usually very lonely."

I don't care for relationships that start out with tricks to prove your love. I can't stand women who say, "Do it for me." I remember my mother saying that so often, and I always came out on the losing side. "Go argue with your father for me," or "Don't argue with your father." "Eat up all the fish," or "Give the fish to your sister." I never ask for any proof of love. I'm satisfied with words.

61

Frank was a tall, skinny fellow, rather lanky, the sort who would have been an excellent basketball player, if it weren't for the fact that he detested sports. He seemed obsessed with the war in Europe, although from what I gathered during that lunch, a fistula of the spine had kept him out of the war in Vietnam and out of every other thing that had no connection with his total dedication to cybernetics. And to Eva. Cybernetics has never been my forte, so our conversation gave every indication of being slightly limited. Fortunately, on my work-related trips to the United States I had learned one word that's indispensable in a conversation with any type of North American—man or woman—no matter what their age, marital status or social class. I found that I could hold an entire conversation with Frank, thanks to the word, "fine." My work was "fine," the city I lived in, in Europe, was "fine," the meal was "fine," Eva was "fine," I was "fine" myself, and life, everything, in and of itself, was "fine"; in spite of the war in Europe, famine in Africa, rape, murder, cancer, AIDS and adultery. Frank was "fine" too. He even gave me permission to smoke after lunch. (Frank did not drink alcohol, or smoke. I, on the other hand, smoked, and I loved meat. Red meat, bloody, sensual, appetizing, pungent, fatty and full of protein. And cigarette smoke. A bluish smoke, packed with nicotine, that always stimulated the cerebral connections and desire.)

We finally finished our coffee, and Frank got up to leave. Although you wouldn't think it, he worked at an office. I had imagined him doing it all from his favorite armchair in the middle of the living room: investing in the stock market, designing super-fast chips, cooking hamburgers, reading the newspaper and making love with

Eva.

"It's been a real pleasure meeting you," he said, holding out his hand to me. "Eva was right," he added: "You're a very attractive, very intelligent woman."

This last observation left me dumbfounded. I made an effort to look at his face very intently, searching for some revealing sign: complicity with Eva, mockery, irony, but his face (small in relation to his height) expressed an innocent normalcy that puzzled me. Either he was stupid (which was difficult to believe, in any case) or he was extremely intelligent.

As soon as he closed the door, I sounded out Eva: "What did you tell him, for God's sake?" I asked.

"The truth," Eva answered with apparent naiveté.

"What kind of truth?" I shouted, horrified.

"That you are attractive and intelligent, and that you have a wonderful sense of humor," declared Eva.

Her reply did not relieve my uncertainty.

"Every time you meet an attractive, intelligent woman, do you bring her home and introduce her to your husband?" I asked in astonishment.

I immediately realized that this question was as ambiguous as the relationship between the two of them.

"Of course not," she defended herself. "But this time it's different. I couldn't help talking about you, while you were in Washington. In fact," she added, "that was the only thing I could talk about. I think Frank got jealous. So I decided that the best thing was to have the two of you meet."

"The best thing for what?" I asked, in a daze.

"So that we could spend the whole week undisturbed," Eva responded. "I told him that there's another convention in New York, and that I'll stay at the hotel. So I won't have to drive back, exhausted, at who knows what ungodly hour."

"Did he believe you?" I asked anxiously.

"Why shouldn't he?" answered Eva in exasperation.

The second most wonderful week of our lives flew by as quickly as the first one, if that's possible, and with the same passion. Only people who have never experienced true physical attraction would be capable of saying that physical attraction is just one part of love, and not the most important part. As far as how important it was, Eva and I were in complete agreement.

We didn't talk about anything personal that was coming up. If the conversations of people in love were recorded, they would turn out to be absolutely stupid. On the other hand, if their looks were filmed, that would reveal their pleasure. A pleasure for which there are no words but the trivial ones: "I love your hair," "Suck me," "Touch me," "Drink me," "Hold me," "I love your belly," things like that.

There was never any risk of meeting anyone we knew; during the second most wonderful week of our lives, we seldom left the hotel suite on Lexington Avenue, and when we did, it was always after midnight, for a cup of coffee (the best thing about New York City is that you can get a cup of coffee at any hour of the day or night), gaze at St. Patrick's Cathedral all lighted up, or listen to old jazz records at a store filled with extremely nice gays. Although we seldom left the hotel suite on Lexington Avenue, we had made some plans. They concerned the future, the word that's forbidden in all dictionaries of reality. Our jobs gave us a great deal of freedom of time and place, so it was easy to find a point we would have in common. Eva loathed Europe, but she was willing to spend a certain amount of time (six months, let's say) in Brussels, where we could both rent an apartment while we worked at our respective jobs. It sounded easy, enjoyable and without any great complications.

On Friday, as night was falling, I left the hotel room for a moment to buy some records that I had ordered that morning.

"Don't be long," Eva had said while I listened to the water from the shower that was beginning to trickle down over her body, shiny with perspiration.

I was not long. I returned innocently to the hotel, with my plastic bag and the records in my hand, but as I walked toward the elevator, a young bellhop holding an enormous bouquet of flowers in his arms stopped me:

"I think these are for you," he told me. "I was going to take them up to your room."

Surprised, I took the bouquet, and let the elevator go on by. I thought of Eva: perhaps she had taken advantage of my absence to offer me this unexpected gift. I opened the perfumed yellow card, and read: *"I'll wait for you at the bar."* It wasn't Eva's handwriting or her style. Confused, I walked quickly to the hotel bar with its coral blue taffeta wall covering. A pianist was playing songs of the fifties while a tall, thin, blond girl was singing in a mellow voice, full of nostalgia. I had the sensation of being in another time, in another place. The bar was nearly empty, so I had no trouble spotting Frank, sitting on one of those horrible metal swivel stools, facing the door so that he could watch the guests as they went up or down in the three hotel elevators, next to each other. I assumed that he was waiting for me, but I didn't know if it was only me he was expecting. I didn't know either if, before he saw me, he had found out that Eva was staying at the hotel or if, in a bold move, he had asked for the number of our room. When he saw me, he waved at me from a distance, spontaneously and cordially. Whatever it was, I had to confront it and try to protect Eva: she might still be showering in the room, naively. That was a possibility, although I wasn't very sure.

"Hello," Frank greeted me, waving his glass.

He was having an orange drink. Something healthy and full of vitamins, I guessed.

"A whiskey," I ordered. "With a lot of ice."

"Did you like the flowers?" Frank asked me.

I had set them down to one side, on the metal barstool, with about as much gracefulness as you might a crippled man's pair of crutches.

"They're very pretty," I said. "Thank you. But I don't understand…"

"Today is Friday," Frank interrupted. "You've finished a week's work at the conference, haven't you? I thought you might like to celebrate. In spite of the fact that you don't like New York," said Frank. "Maybe New Yorkers are a little more to your liking than the city is," he insinuated.

My God, what a klutz he was. I didn't know men well enough to know if it was a klutziness of their *gender*, or if it was a subjective personal kind, all his own.

I kept quiet, taking a drink of whiskey, because he took up the thread again.

"I have a couple tickets to the theater on

66

Broadway. I thought you might like to see a show before you left."

I detest musicals, and I detest the theater. Eva knew that. Frank didn't.

"I'm really tired," I told him. "I appreciate the flowers, you were very kind. But I would rather not go out tonight."

He seemed to be disappointed. But I wasn't sure if it was because I had turned him down, or if it was another kind of disappointment. Now I had to try to make him leave before Eva got the brilliant idea of coming down to wait for me in the lobby, or of having them page me. (She had already done that once, while I was reading the newspaper on a settee next to the reception desk.)

I drank the rest of my whiskey in one swallow, and seized the moment to tell him:

"I'd like to treat you to a drink now, Frank, but I'm expecting a long-distance phone call in my room, and I don't want to miss it."

Frank looked into the bottom of his glass where a few bubbles were still floating, and blurted out:

"Do you know where Eva is?"

The surprise of it made me sit back down. Badly done. I should have remained on my feet, with the flowers under my arm, to get out of there as fast as I could.

I hesitated. There were all sorts of possible answers—all of them false—and I needed to choose one, quickly.

"I don't know," I answered, trying to sound sincere.

He avoided my eyes.

"It's nothing important," he said. "She hasn't

called me this week," he added. "It often happens when her conference work has her tied up. You know," he continued, "she's an obsessive worker. I don't mean that as criticism," he quickly clarified. "I'm obsessive about my work too. We're an odd couple," he said. "Two compulsive workers. I thought that today, it being Friday, I might find her home tonight, but she hasn't come."

"The discussions most likely have gone overtime," I said.

"Yes," said Frank. "That's why I thought I might use the tickets I had for the theater and invite you. I don't think Eva would mind," he added.

"No, I don't think so," I said very seriously.

I took a quick glance at the bar's revolving door that opened onto the hotel lobby. I had to have some words ready just in case, suddenly, splendidly, exhibiting her flamboyant and indisputable sexual satisfaction, Eva should appear. Although it was quite possible that those intelligent phrases would occur to her much more quickly than they would to me.

"Has she told you anything about our marriage?" Frank asked unexpectedly.

I thought he had made this trip to the hotel just to ask me that question. He had driven from New Jersey, faint-hearted and frightened of the traffic, the pollution, the crime, frightened for Eva, for the war in Europe, for the world's future, just to be able to ask me this question that I was not going to answer honestly, of course.

"I'm not a marriage expert," I answered, trying to be evasive.

One of the elevators had just come down, and the metal doors opened, allowing dozens of men and women to come pouring out. I tried to look over Frank's shoulder. Why was this guy so damn tall?

"I know that," said Frank.

I detected a certain irritability in the tone of his voice. He was right: the reply had been too evasive.

"I have problems," Frank confessed.

Now I couldn't use that stupid stock phrase: And who doesn't? In the elevator that just came down, Eva had not appeared. Hopefully she was entertaining herself, watching a video or listening to a music cassette. Unfortunately, I thought, her greatest entertainment, all week long, had been me. She was going to notice my absence all too soon.

"It's not the first time it's happened," said Frank.

I didn't know what he was talking about. It might be his own problems, it could be something else.

"It's happened a number of times over the course of our marriage," he added. He asked for another orange drink, the way a person would ask for a glass of whiskey or hemlock, so that he could commit suicide: "All of a sudden," he said, "Eva loses interest. She starts behaving oddly."

"Do you mean her trips?" I asked. "The job she has…"

"I don't mean that," Frank answered calmly. "Eva is free to do anything she wants to: that was the condition of our marriage. I'm free too," he added. "It's a political pact, to put it one way."

"Does that freedom include silence?" I asked.

If Frank was in no mood to let me go, and something in his determination, in his demeanor and even in the set of his legs made me fear him, I had to try to involve myself in the matter in some way, even if it was to get some sort of information. Just so long as he believed me. Did he believe me?

"That's just it. If she's free, why doesn't she tell me anything? I ought to know. It doesn't seem right to me that her lady friends should know, and that I don't."

It was the first time that Frank had used the plural, speaking of Eva's female friends. I confess that it alarmed me a little.

"What lady friends?" I asked, making a show of innocence.

"You and the others," said Frank.

"Eva has never mentioned any other lady friends to me," I said. "Maybe because we haven't known each other very long."

"Excuse me," he said (sincerely?). "I forgot that you're the most recent one."

I swear that at that moment I wished I were the very first one.

"She must have talked about it to someone else," Frank reasoned, but it didn't sound to me like he was very convinced. "Even so," he added, "it doesn't seem right that she doesn't discuss it with me."

"Maybe she doesn't have anything to tell you," I offered as an excuse.

For the first time, Frank looked directly into my eyes. It was odd because he had only been drinking orange juice, and to my knowledge orange juice doesn't bring out that sort of sheen in anyone's look.

"She wouldn't tell me, no matter what," said Frank. "That's what she gets off on," he asserted sententiously, very sure of himself.

I was silent for a moment, thinking about his words. Then I leaned over the bar, toward him, and I asked:

"These flowers, were they for her?"

"Yes, admitted Frank. "She likes me to give her surprises once in a while, and I think that lately I've neglected her a little. I've been very busy with my work."

He stood up. Now two elevators had come down to the lobby at the same time. He did not look in their direction.

"They're very pretty, " I said evenly.

"I don't want to bother you any further," added Frank. "You deserve a good rest."

His statement sounded as ambivalent to me as all the rest of the conversation.

"If she calls you, or if you see her," said Frank, "I'd appreciate it if you wouldn't tell her anything about our meeting here. I like to have my secrets too," he finished, and put out his hand.

I seldom shake hands with a man. I don't know why, but it just never occurs to me.

Frank left without a glance at the elevators.

Even though he had the courtesy to pay the bill, I still called the bartender over. I had gone out to the street without a pen, something that a good secretary should never do. The bartender gave me a pen and a blank card that I asked him for. I wrote: "For Eva. With love. From Frank," and I attached it to the flowers, just the way the first card had been.

"Take them up to room 823," I told the doorman, and I gave him a ten-dollar bill.

I had another whiskey at the bar while I waited, the

way it happens in the movies. I've seen hundreds of films that are set in New York. New York is a city that I like much better in movies than I do in real life.

After a while, I went up to the room.

As I had imagined, Eva was watching a music program on the television. Elton John, a musician she liked. I liked him too. I didn't see the flowers anywhere. They weren't in the bedroom or in the upper level of the suite. Had she thrown them in the trash? I took the lid off the trash can, but I didn't find them there either.

"You were gone a long time," Eva told me, without turning off the TV. "What were you doing?"

"I was talking to Frank," I said with feigned innocence.

It was one of those moments when Elton John, completely swept up, was pressing the keyboard with the same soft intensity with which one would caress a woman's body.

"You're very funny," Eva remarked, still holding onto the remote control.

I began to pack my bag. I usually travel very light. I would like to be wealthy and buy what I need in the cities where I stay.

"He's anxious because you've been gone so long," I told her. "Even though I think he knows perfectly well where you are and with whom."

"That's impossible," said Eva.

Elton John was playing a sweet and final arpeggio that brought an ovation from the audience.

"I think he bought tickets to the theater," I continued. "At least, that's what he told me."

"I'm sure he wanted to go with you," commented

Eva, unperturbed.

Now, on the TV screen, a recital by Pavarotti was beginning.

"I don't go to the theater with strangers," I answered.

She hadn't noticed, but my suitcase was all set.

"What are you doing?" she asked in astonishment, when she realized that I was about to leave.

"I don't care much for New York," I answered. "I definitely do not like it," I said, and I reached the door.

At that moment I saw the flowers. They were tossed on the floor, carelessly, under the bed. It wasn't right, for the flowers.

# A DELICATE CONSULTATION

"Dress up," Dr. Minnovis murmured to his patient, a powerful executive in the dairy industry.

Dr. Minnovis was a psychologist. As a young man he had wanted to study Engineering, but since he wasn't accepted in that school at the university, he chose Psychology. Then—at twenty years of age—he imagined a future wearing a white coat, in an office within the narrow halls of the Insurance Building, where he would have to listen to hordes of women suffering from vague, undefined afflictions of a hazy nature, to whom he would prescribe tranquilizers. Tranquilizers from different laboratories, but of a similar composition. The female patients would anxiously ask: "How many pills should I take?" And he would indicate a moderate dosage: not too many and not too few. Tranquilizers for making marriage bearable, tranquilizers for household chores, tranquilizers for sexual boredom, in short, tranquilizers for living. Placebos for a unique malaise, that of living. When things can't be changed (and Dr. Minnovis thought that most things could not be changed), you had to prescribe tranquilizers.

The future wasn't much different from what he had thought it would be (Dr. Minnovis was a normal man: that is, one with scant imagination). Instead of finding a position with the Office of Social Security (there were few of those: the State did not think it worthwhile to spend money on vague, incurable disorders), he got a steady job with a Businessmen's Mutual. It was an association of business men and women who had their own healthcare service. Wealthy men with fine houses, nice automobiles, beautiful wives, trips abroad, children who were studying for their Master's degree at universities in the U. S., and with magnificent homes in the country or at the beach. He had a light schedule (he only went in for a couple of hours, three times a week), and he had very little work. The business men and women had all sorts of ways at their disposal to combat boredom or stress; they seldom went to see Dr. Minnovis. In the first five years of his tenure, he only had to deal with a couple cases of depression, because of commercial failures, because of an occasional investment that had gone bad, and one case of melancholic depression that turned out to be due to a heavy addiction to cocaine. All these cases were taken care of in a few weekly sessions, and Dr. Minnovis never saw the patients again.

Mr. Enríquez had asked for his first appointment one month before, and during that period they met three times. Mr. Enríquez was a skilled industrialist. He was forty years old, married, the father of two children who were studying abroad, and was in good health. He bought his shirts and ties at an Italian store, ate at the finest restaurants, and liked to take the helm of his own yacht. As he said on his first visit, everything was normal. But Mr. Enríquez felt *perturbed*. (Does perturbed come from *turbulence*? wondered Dr. Minnovis. A muddy black slick that rises from the bottom to the surface. Loch Ness is a lake of turbulence. Perhaps that's why people believe in the existence of a monster. They think it's there, even though they're not able to catch sight of it. A monster of turbulence. If it exists, thought Dr. Minnovis, it's a turbulent monster, like all monsters. What does it matter whether it's in or out of water? Everything is in and out at the same time, Dr. Minnovis told himself.)

Mr. Enríquez was speaking slowly and deliberately, as though he were having some problem. But the problem was not in his vocal cords: it was more in the very sap of the language. In his notebook Dr. Minnovis jotted down that the patient's grasp of language was cultivated, but that his manner of speaking indicated a state of deep-seated anxiety. ("Deep-seated," wrote Dr. Minnovis: submerged, like the most important impulses.) After three sessions Dr. Minnovis had not been able to uncover the reasons for Mr. Enríquez's apparent depression. They must be imaginary. People suffer more for imaginary reasons than for real ones. Mr. Enríquez's marriage was all right (as good as any other, thought Dr. Minnovis), and he had no economic problems. Nor had he recently lost a loved one.

Nonetheless, Mr. Enríquez had *confessed* (that was the right word: a painful, intimate, nearly unendurable confession) that he harbored a secret doubt: he wasn't certain, deep down, if he was a man or a woman. It wasn't a matter of any physical confusion. Mr. Enríquez knew that he *looked like* a man. There was nothing about his body that would lead him to suspect anything else. He had a hefty physique, he exercised, he was an excellent swimmer, his virile member was potent, and he had never had any episodes of impotence. But in spite of all that, Mr. Enríquez often felt that he was a woman. He couldn't tell anyone about it. He was afraid of appearing ridiculous. During *all those years* he had kept this feeling to himself ("How many years?" Dr. Minnovis asked in a deliberately

76

impenetrable tone of voice. *"Many, too many,"* murmured the patient) until he felt like the sensation was suffocating him: from a feeling it had turned into an emotion, into a trial, affirmed Mr. Enríquez. Even so, he had hesitated a long while before deciding to consult a psychologist. It was something he hadn't wanted to reveal to anyone, although, on the other hand, he felt an urgent need to do so.

Dr. Minnovis listened to him, perplexed. There was nothing in the patient's appearance, in his habits or in his past that would lead him to think that there could be any conflict of sexual identity. Besides, these conflicts, no matter how delusional they might be, usually appear at a young age, seldom in someone who is forty years old.

"It's very strange not to be certain about who you are," said Mr. Enríquez, with obvious effort.

Dr. Minnovis wrote down the word "certain" in his notebook. He tried to hold back a look of irritation, and perhaps that was the reason he was somewhat tolerant.

"In a certain sense," he said, as if he were dealing with a student and not with a patient, although sometimes it was difficult to separate the two, "certainties are imaginary. Constructs of fantasy. One man begins to believe that he's God, and he begins to talk like a visionary. Another man thinks his ideas can change the world, and he rallies together a band of revolutionaries. Some think their hands have the power of healing, and people with incurable illnesses line up to see them. The opposite of certainty," continued Dr. Minnovis, "is a reasonable doubt, only a *reasonable* one," he insisted, "that does not cause too much anguish."

Mr. Enríquez was an intelligent person.

"Do you mean that the problem is in my *idea* of being a man, and not in reality?" he asked. "And yet," he added uneasily, before Dr. Minnovis had time to answer, "I'm talking about a *feeling*, not an idea."

Dr. Minnovis wrote the word "feeling" in his notebook. Occasionally in his free time—and he had a good deal of that—he thought he might use those notes to write something. A novel, or perhaps an essay. But he was too lazy.

"I meant that most certainties are delusions, and one can get along without them." Dr. Minnovis thought it best to speak very firmly and insistently. The challenge of giving the patient "emotional support" sometimes did not rest on what was said so much as the tone of voice in which it was said. Anyone who asks for a consultation with a psychologist is someone who needs help, and help is not a concept; it could be a gesture, an attitude, the inflection of one's voice. "It's possible to live with a reasonable number of doubts," continued Dr. Minnovis. "If I may, I'll tell you, and *only on a philosophical level*, you understand: it's not good to think about problems that you're in no position to resolve."

Mr. Enríquez had begun to talk, and now he seemed more inclined to go on than to listen.

"It doesn't depend on whether I'm willing or not," explained the patient. "It's not an *idea*," he repeated. "It's a feeling, and there's nothing I can do to stop it from coming on. The *feeling* that I'm a woman takes me by surprise, suddenly and unexpectedly, sometimes at the most awkward times. Then I *feel* that inside me there's a crouching, hidden woman, pleading to come out, a repressed woman. A woman who can't bring herself to

78

make an appearance, to come out into the public light."

Dr. Minnovis repressed an urge to show his annoyance. Listening to his patient was irritating him. He felt like shaking him, beating him, teaching him a *lesson*. Dr. Minnovis was taken aback. Was he feeling like a father, confronting the sexual doubts of a capricious, adolescent son? He tried not to show that in any way, and he asked in a noncommittal tone of voice:

"Do you remember the last time it happened? Can you describe it?"

Now Mr. Enríquez seemed to be more at ease, as if he had understood that the psychologist's query was a prodding, an overture. (A very feminine interpretation, Dr. Minnovis jotted down in his notebook.)

"It happened to me a few days ago, when I was at a business meeting. There were five or six of us executives, and we were discussing a contract for a large supermarket in the outskirts of the city. We had taken care of the initial difficulties, and the deal was nearly complete. We celebrated the agreement by having a few drinks in a fashionable spot before lunch. Suddenly I looked at our group and thought: 'I'm the only woman at this meeting.' It was very strange because I was thinking this at the same time that I was talking to the others about a section in the contract. No one noticed, but I began to feel like my voice was changing, and that I needed to cross my legs in a very feminine way. I didn't do it, of course. But when one of my colleagues tipped a glass of whiskey over on the table, I told myself: 'My blouse is going to get stained. I'll have to go to the washroom, and I'll take a minute to touch up my hair.' As it happened, the little accident did stain my shirt, but I didn't go to the washroom. I was afraid to go into the ladies' room. I would have felt ridiculous. But I still kept thinking about the blouse. I felt a soft brushing against my tits…"

"That was all just your imagination," interrupted Dr. Minnovis, slightly annoyed.

The patient protested:

"No, Doctor," he said. "It isn't my imagination: sometimes I really *feel* like a woman."

Dr. Minnovis turned in his chair. He was beginning to *feel* violent.

"And how do you know what it is, *to feel* like a woman?" he asked impatiently.

Mr. Enríquez was silent; he seemed to be thinking. Then he lifted his head and looked directly into his eyes.

"Do you know?" he asked anxiously.

"No," said the doctor. "I don't know what a woman feels like, because I'm a man," he answered firmly.

"What would you say if at some moment you began to feel a little bit like a woman?" the patient asked him.

Dr. Minnovis suppressed a sigh. The problem with obsessions was their rebelliousness. A little obsession, of no importance at first, begins to swell up like a pregnancy. It's a hypertrophic fetus that is not disgorged after nine months; sometimes it is never disgorged; perhaps some day scientists will come up with a pill for obsessions; in the meantime, one would have to struggle as best he could.

"That's impossible," he answered. "I couldn't begin to feel like a woman, as you say, for the plain and simple reason that I'm a man, just like you are."

"Do you *feel* like a man all the time?" asked the

patient, genuinely curious.

"I never wonder about that," answered the psychologist. "Those are things that, once they've been established, don't require any further investigation. And just so you won't forget it," he added with a severity that he thought was more therapeutic than the words themselves, "I'll tell you that a human being's sexual identity is established at birth, according to their genital organs and their chromosomes. It is objective data. Sexual activity is something else. We can do whatever we like with our genital organs, but that doesn't call into question our sexual identity."

"I'm not talking about my genitals," the patient was quick to respond. "I have no doubts at all about them," he continued. "To me, it seems like that sensation, that feeling I told you about, pursues me independently from my genital organs."

Dr. Minnovis picked up a letter-opener, shaped like a knife, that he used for opening his mail. The electric bill, the telephone bill, medical advertisements.

"Being a man or being a woman is not an *idea*, my dear fellow," he muttered, almost indignant. "Genitals don't appertain to ideas, they're a part of reality."

One had to combat obsessions with strong doses of reality. Reality: something that no one liked completely.

"Do you mean that my ideas, my feelings are an illusion, that they're imaginary?" the patient asked in dismay.

The doctor did not want this *idea* (to think that he was insane) to worry the patient. It was enough for him to *believe* he was a woman; he didn't need to *believe* he was a crazy woman, on top of that. It was a case of depression.

81

Severe depression, with elements of delirium. It might have to do with age, with a mid-life crisis, and hormonal metabolism. Chemical imbalances that bring on hallucinations.

Dr. Minnovis and Mr. Enríquez were the same age. In a way, the doctor thought, he too was going through a crisis, a time of slight depression, although not with the elements of delirium his patient had. His own crisis revealed itself in a certain lassitude, a slight letdown; the sense of having wasted a good part of his life. He had been married for many years. And during those years he had had a few extramarital relationships. Things that didn't amount to a *hill of beans* (Maybe what he really needed was another kind of *hill.*) But he had never been enthralled. Not with a woman, not with an idea, not with his work. While carrying on his practice he had learned, more graphically than in books, to shy away from passions, with all their destructive power. Now he began to wonder if that had been the correct course. He had always felt proud of his ability to remain aloof, of his self-control, but instead of being a virtue it might be a matter of lacking something, of a shortcoming.

"Put on a disguise," Dr. Minnovis advised his patient, out of the blue.

It was a provocative statement, but he thought it was a good time to change strategy. Sometimes the unexpected had a therapeutic effect on patients.

"What do you mean?" asked Mr. Enríquez, alarmed.

"Simply that," insisted the doctor. "Disguise yourself once in a while. Buy some women's clothes and put them on when you're all by yourself. You don't need to go out in public or cause a scandal. A solitary, private act, yours and yours alone. In that way, it could be that the 'idea' may disappear. When there's a realization that it's able to reveal itself, when you give freedom to the woman you *think* you have inside, it will stop pursuing you. It won't need to sneak around, hiding. Give free rein to your desire," advised Dr. Minnovis.

The man sat there, startled. Not just by the psychologist's suggestion, but by his change in attitude. He had noticed a certain unconscious irritation in him, as if the doctor had to make an effort to control his aggression. But when he said, "Give free rein to your desire," Mr. Enríquez believed he saw that the statement was not addressed just to him, but to the world in general. However, it was a matter of a belief, and recently he had decided not to trust his beliefs.

"Am I to infer," he asked cautiously, "that you think the idea that is haunting and troubling me is in reality a hidden, repressed desire?"

"Most of our ideas and 'beliefs,'" explained the doctor, "are desires in *disguise*."

"And when I put on a *disguise*, I would reveal myself, even if that's a paradox?" asked the patient.

"Don't worry about it," the doctor sighed. "Disguises are liberating: the play that they set in motion reduces the tension between reality and desire."

There was silence. Mr. Enríquez seemed to be lost in thought, as though he was weighing the pros and cons, the expediency of a business transaction, a contract for something.

"I don't know if I'll be able to bear it if I know what my desire is," he admitted fearfully.

"Quite possibly you will discover that it's not what you're afraid of," said the doctor. "A person thinks he is looking for one thing, and he finds something else, or when he finds what he's looking for he realizes that that isn't it at all."

"The desire to be a woman is something very *feminine*," the patient protested.

"Don't you believe it," responded Dr. Minnovis. "Most women would like to be men. Besides, categorizing desires according to one's sex is a neurotic, emasculating practice. You shouldn't even think about it."

"I've *constructed* my life as a man," reflected Mr. Enríquez.

"Those are always *constructions*, even if we aren't fully aware of them," pointed out the doctor. "If there are no fissures," he added, "it's possible to never be aware of that."

"I'm afraid," confessed the patient.

"Being afraid doesn't always protect you," responded Dr. Minnovis. "Sometimes it's a hindrance, it defers, dissuades or nullifies."

It seemed to him that they had gotten to the bottom of the matter. Supposing that there was a bottom. It could be that it was a false bottom, a bottom that was a screen, and that it might be hiding another bottom underneath.

But Mr. Enríquez, always doubtful, insisted once more:

"What do you think I would achieve by doing that?"

"Perhaps the realization that being a woman is a failure too," declared Dr. Minnovis, and he ended the session.

Mr. Enríquez never returned. Dr. Minnovis thought that possibly he had been shocked by his suggestion, and that being frightened had therapeutic effects: he had taught him to feel at ease with his obsession. In any case, it wasn't his practice to follow his patients once they stopped coming.

Meanwhile, spring had arrived. An unsettled spring. There were very windy days, and others that were calm but with grey skies. Pollen was very thick in the air. Like many people, Dr. Minnovis began to suffer from allergies.

Midway through spring, Mr. Minnovis and his wife separated. He felt an intense need to be alone. Surely, it was only a passing stage, but he decided to do it. It could be the final crisis in his life, and he had to take advantage of it. Those crises, despite their anguish and pain, offer a ruthless look at one's inner-self. He rented a discreet bachelor's apartment in a nice neighborhood, maid service and laundry included. As soon as he did this, he felt a comforting sense of relief. He would go to work at the Businessmen's Mutual, take a walk, and when he returned to his apartment he would make a sandwich, drink a glass of milk, and spend the rest of the time by himself, in pleasant relaxation. He liked to be alone, without any ties, as if he were the only inhabitant in the world. He listened to the messages on his answering machine in the evening, but hardly ever returned the calls. Sometimes he fell asleep on the living room sofa, with the T.V. on. He would occasionally watch some classic black and white movie or pornographic shorts, and these acted like a soporific for him. Dr. Minnovis had a sense that his libido had fallen off considerably, but that discovery did not trouble him. In the same way that many people take vacations during their lives to do things they have never done before, he felt it was fitting that he should take a vacation from doing what he had done all his life.

He did not make love, but one afternoon, after strolling through a shopping center with large department stores, Dr. Minnovis went into an elegant shop of feminine lingerie. His eyes fell on a black brassiere covered with lace, with a clasp, not in back but between the breasts. When he pressed the little hook, the two cups of the brassiere sprang apart with a distinct snap. Dr. Minnovis thought it a very amusing little device. When the clasp separated, it was like opening huge floodgates. The breasts spilled out in all their glory. He was also attracted by some shiny red silk tights, with only one opening at the height of the vulva. He had them package up both items, and asked for gift-wrapping.

He did not have Mr. Enríquez's address: he had left it back at the office.

That evening Dr. Minnovis decided to dine alone, in his bachelor's apartment. He had bought fresh vegetables, fish, and a bottle of good wine. For dessert, cheesecake with raspberries.

He lit a candle for an intimate dinner, put a recording with the deep voice of Dionne Warwick on the phonograph, and when the music stopped he lit a cigarette. He no longer smoked the way he used to, but on special occasions he rewarded himself with a cigarette. The night was pleasant, no question about that. He went over to the glass-enclosed balcony and looked out at the enormous sign of the Philips Company in the distance, going around and around in the dark sky, with its intense red and yellow lights. The parabolic antennae of the buildings, sticking up like crosses, looked like the religious symbols of some authoritarian civilization. Then, slowly, Dr. Minnovis made up his mind to unwrap the lingerie he had bought.

When he put them on, he was astonished to see that he could easily work the fastenings on the clasps and belts. That only proved that men's clumsiness with women's clothing was not clumsiness at all: it was a defense mechanism to keep others, or one's self, from being confused.

His reflection in the mirror, dressed in a black, lacy brassiere with large breast cups, and garters of the same color, with his rigid male sex protruding from between his legs, seemed to him like an ad in a pornographic magazine. He smiled, and immediately felt a delightful sensation of pleasure. No one was looking at him, he could do whatever he liked without witnesses, without judges, with no one to criticize him. And what Dr. Minnovis wanted to do, that night, was caress his breasts, which were enormous, cover them with his fingers, glide down to his thighs, dance, dance, like a chorus girl, while Dionne Warwick, on the CD, was murmuring: "How Lovely to Be a Woman."

# STRANGE CIRCUMSTANCES

For her husband to die unexpectedly, at the age of thirty-eight, and without having been ill, was not the most painful part to Josefina, in spite of the fact that she had two small children and an uncertain economic road ahead. What troubled her most were the circumstances of her husband's death.

That was it: Javier Martín, thirty-eight years old, owner of a small textile factory with twenty-five employees, had died under "strange circumstances," according to the press. The newspapers added that he had died in a room at the rear of the factory: a private room where he apparently spent his free time, far from the machinery and workshops. Josefina had never heard about that room; she didn't even know it existed. True enough, she generally didn't go to the factory. She was too busy with the children, the housework, and besides she wasn't at all interested in the textile industry. Javier hadn't mentioned that room or any other one to her either, because when he got home after a long day's work, he had no desire to talk about business.

Two policemen came to her door to bring her the news of her husband's death, while the children (a girl, five years old, and a boy, eight) were at school. The policemen seemed to be nervous; they showed their identification and then, somewhat self-consciously, told her that her husband had died "under strange circumstances." She immediately thought it was a

88

homicide. A horrible murder, for money, or something to do with business. Times were hard. The economic crisis had taken its toll on so many companies and had ruined the industry. Several factories had closed down, workers were unemployed. Banks wouldn't offer credit, and if they did, the interest rates were so high that people in business couldn't pay them. But the policemen, who seemed to be rather reticent, or suspicious (in her confusion when she heard the news, Josefina wasn't able to see things clearly), assured her that her husband had not been murdered. "An accident," she thought. Maybe one of the machines at the shop. Her husband had tried to repair it, and the machine had caused his death. Or a furnace. A furnace had exploded and burned the place down. But the police told her that it had been a different kind of accident. The accident had nothing to do with work. "Then it was the car. It was so foggy on the road that he crashed into a tree, or he lost control when the car skidded on the ice." But none of these things seemed to have caused her husband's death either. The police told her that in a certain sense he had brought on his own death. This information startled Josefina so much that she staggered back, leaned against a chair and felt like she was going to faint. She asked for a glass of water. One of the policemen looked around, took a few steps, and finally went to the kitchen and brought her a glass of water from the tap. The water had the taste of chlorine that's so common in big cities. She never used that water for drinking or for cooking. She drank feverishly, as if it had been centuries since she'd had anything to drink. What reason could Javier have to commit suicide? It's true that business wasn't flourishing at the moment, but the small factory had weathered the crisis by specializing in printed T-shirts, and her husband was an optimist, he never got discouraged. As for their marriage, it was going along as usual. Not passionately, but harmoniously. They had been married for ten years, and they hadn't had any major disagreements. Her husband loved the children very much (especially the little one, Alicia), and they didn't cause any problems. "A mistress," thought Josefina. Maybe her husband had a mistress on the sly, and he hadn't been able to take the pressure of the deception. She dismissed that idea: Javier was a solid man, he wouldn't go off the deep end. He might have had a lover, but in that case it would have been the woman who was the victim, not him. And if the situation was more serious—if Javier wanted another wife, for example—he would have automatically taken its measure, like a good businessman, thinking through the pros and cons of a divorce.

Finally, one of the policemen let drop that her husband had died of suffocation from a plastic bag. This information did nothing to diminish Josefina's perplexity. What was her husband doing with a plastic bag over his head? Javier wasn't a reckless man. She could think of no reason why he should be fooling around with a plastic bag, unless he had decided to commit suicide. The policeman insisted that it wasn't a case of suicide, although, in a way, it was an involuntary suicide. She didn't find this explanation at all convincing. There are many cases of unsuccessful suicides, because the person simply craves attention, wants to show how tormented he is, wants to make demands. But very few people who want to live, end up committing suicide.

Finally, the other policeman revealed that her

husband had died, suffocated by a plastic bag while wearing a lacy, black garter and matching brassiere, and with a pair of broaches fastened to his nipples. In his mouth was an orange, only slightly bitten. Not far away was a three-pronged whip. There were marks on his body that showed that, before he died, he had lashed himself, not too hard, but possibly just to excite himself.

Josefina felt like her nerves were coming apart like a ball of yarn. The other policeman's cold, blunt description made her laugh at first, then burst into tears, hysterically. The first policeman told her it would do her good to cry a little, and then he quickly added that it was late, and he was sorry, but she needed to go with them *to the scene of the incident*. If she wished, she could call a relative so that she wouldn't feel entirely alone. The magistrate in charge of the case was in a hurry, it had been such a trying day. He also informed her that there was a police car parked outside to take her there.

She couldn't think of anyone to call. Who could she call? Her parents lived far away from the city, and besides, she didn't want to upset them. Josefina remembered that her husband had a lawyer for the factory's business affairs, contracts, sales, things of that sort. She didn't think it would be proper to call him for something like this.

The magistrate handling the matter was not a man, but rather a woman. A young lady who had just graduated from university, she supposed, and who had passed the bar after cramming day and night. She seemed to be rather bewildered, although she tried to hide it, the same way Josefina was doing. It had to be one of her very first cases.

When Josefina arrived at *the scene of the incident*,

as the police called it, the lady-magistrate informed her that they had already drawn up a report, but that she needed to identify the body and sign a receipt. Josefina thought a dead man was like a piece of merchandise: something that's delivered against the signature of the buyer. But she had not bought her husband's body. It belonged to her, just the same, the way his clothing belonged to her, the objects in his office, and even his debts, but she was an involuntary owner. The magistrate advised her to call her husband's lawyer; and one of the factory employees—someone she didn't know, but who had been observing everything from a distance, with a desire to step in—offered to make the call. Finding herself involved in a process that she found embarrassing and absurd, to say the least, Josefina asked if she should go *into the scene of the incident* to identify her husband in the same circumstances that they had found him, and the magistrate answered yes, but that it was a very brief process, and she needn't take a long time looking. The mortuary would handle everything else.

When Josefina entered the factory's mysterious back room, she had the feeling that she was going into a forbidden place, an intimate, private, secret area. Like the cave of some unknown, ancient, legendary animal, and therefore, dangerous. She also felt that she was violating some unspoken, silent agreement, and wondered if she had a right to do so. She gained access, by chance (as casually as being suffocated by a plastic bag that was only meant to be played with, to intensify one's pleasure), to the temple of a strange religion, one into which she had not been initiated.

That is what it was, in fact: the small room, at the

back of the textile factory, was a sanctuary. But a pagan sanctuary. Even though it was dark—there were no windows or side doors—Josefina could make out the cult figures of that strange religion: leather garments, metal chains, white linens spotted with blood, iron rings hanging from walls, photographs of naked men and women with expressions of mystic or orgasmic exaltation on their faces, red silk, garters of black lace, high women's boots with intertwining drawstrings, small awls, brass belts, large buckles in the shape of a bird or a dog or an eagle, spiky whips, and a set of metal instruments like those she had occasionally seen in the cabinets of medical clinics.

Stretched out on the floor, covered considerately with a white sheet, was her husband's body. Not far away, an empty plastic bag, wrinkled and deflated, held together with clamps. Next to it, an orange, with a shiny, reddish rind—and a small piece bitten out.

Josefina thought she was going to faint, but she made an effort to hold herself together: she didn't want to lose consciousness in that strange room that had been opened for the first and only time for her. She quickly signed the blur of pages they held out to her, facing away from her husband and the strange paraphernalia around him. And yet she knew, beyond a shadow of a doubt, that she would never be able to forget the small, hidden room—like a clandestine operating room—filled with shiny, silky, spiky objects, their metal points, their paper fins. "The playroom of a mad child," she thought. Mad, but unforgettable.

Some days after the funeral, Josefina decided to call a friend. Laura was a journalist for a very modern ladies magazine, for "liberal, independent" women. She had gotten a divorce two years ago, and swore that she would never marry again. She had seen her at the funeral, but only in passing. She thought that she was the only person she would want to talk to. After her husband's death—"under strange circumstances"—Josefina felt a pressing need to talk to someone. "It must be a symptom of hysteria," she told herself, but whatever it was, it was happening to her. An inner voice that continually changed pitch: sometimes it sounded like her own voice, sometimes it sounded like Javier's. But at other times she couldn't recognize it. As though some imaginary person were talking, a nonexistent being that whispered disturbing things in her ear. That wouldn't let her sleep. That kept her awake. Everything it said to her centered around her husband's death. Around his strange sacrifice. That was what the voice called it. Perhaps that voice wanted to speak to her dead husband. Perhaps it was addressing a listener who could not hear or answer it; she could not interrupt it or make it be still. She thought that it was herself, split in two. It was she, wanting to talk to Javier. To shake him. To ask him questions and berate him. She didn't want to talk to her dead husband: she wanted to talk to the living man who wasn't there any longer and couldn't hear her and couldn't answer her, because he was dead, he had unintentionally killed himself, stupidly, with a sad, plastic bag over his head that he hadn't managed to open in time, and with a very red, very dark orange in his mouth, like a breast, like the ideal breast full of milk that a newborn baby sucks on with great delight. She could have continued having a dialogue with the voice that only she could hear, but she thought it wiser to find a listener, someone alive and real. Someone who

94

could break up the continuous soliloquy: "Soli-loquy," she thought: the "solitude" of a "loco"—a madman. Lunatics are completely alone in their lunacy. Her husband shut himself up—alone—in a hidden room to fulfill, perform his games, his erotic ceremonies. Like a madman? Was her husband mad, and she hadn't noticed?

"He wasn't crazy, dear," her friend, Laura, told her firmly. "At least, not completely crazy. No more than you or I."

The local newspapers had published stories about her husband's death on the front page. Her husband wasn't such an important man that he deserved to be on the front page; the "strange circumstances" were, naturally, pure gravy to the reporters. The descriptions contained the most minute details. Not one paper held back the detail about the orange, and as a result one morning her little boy, Javier (he had the same name as his father), asked her:

"Why did Daddy die with an orange in his mouth?"

He must have heard some remark at school; it was inevitable.

"I'm sure it was what he wanted to be doing at the time. He didn't know he was going to die, and he was biting into an orange at that very moment, just the way you chew gum," Josefina explained.

After his father's death, Javier seemed to be in somewhat of a daze. Nothing very significant, just a slight bewilderment.

"And the plastic bag?" asked Javier. "Everybody knows you can't put a plastic bag over your head," he said. "Even little kids know that," he added.

The newspapers had printed a photograph.

95

Fortunately, it was so blurry that you couldn't make anything out very clearly.

"Your father must have been drunk," was the only thing she could think of to tell him. "He had a lot of business meetings," she explained. "He wasn't a drinker, but sometimes, to be sociable, he drank a little too much."

Her son looked at her skeptically. Her answer didn't seem very convincing to him.

"At school they told me that once a little boy put a plastic bag over his head when he was playing, and he suffocated to death," said Javier.

"Adults sometimes behave like children," Josefina thought to say. "And children…, sometimes they behave like adults," she added.

But it couldn't be so broad. The boy wasn't talking about adults: he was talking about his dead father.

"If he suffocated himself with a plastic bag, he must have been an idiot," the boy determined.

She thought that in all his anxiety, Javier had found an explanation. It wasn't a bad tactic: if her son was able to build up a little hostility against his dead father, the pain would subside. That's what Laura said.

"It's really strange that you're not angry at your husband," she admonished her. "The least you can say about him is that he left you in such a rough situation, not to mention an uncomfortable one."

Uncomfortable, the funeral certainly was: all those people talking in hushed tones, looking at her with glances that held compassion and confusion at the same time.

"He didn't do it on purpose," answered Josefina. "He didn't intend to kill himself. He didn't mean to leave me like this. It happened by accident. How can I be mad at him?"

"I think that deep down you feel guilty about something," her friend observed. "It often happens that way. The ideal mother feels guilty about her scatterbrained son's accident, the wife whose husband cheated on her thinks it was her own fault: she didn't give him something, she was inadequate in some way."

"That's possible," Josefina murmured. "If that's it, I hope it won't last long."

The funeral was uncomfortable not only for her. It had been uncomfortable for Javier's parents, and for her own parents too.

"Everyone seems to want to feel sorry about a person who dies of cancer or from a heart attack, or in an airplane accident. But if somebody dies with a plastic bag fastened around his neck and with an orange in his mouth," she told Laura, "the only thing that does is make the people he leaves behind nervous."

"You're forgetting some details," Laura reminded her relentlessly: "the black garters he was wearing and the broaches on his nipples."

That was why she had called her: Josefina felt that she was the only person who could help her. You can't believe everything that comes into your head. You can't believe everything, the way she had the first couple of days. It's best if you believe just a few things, and build some sort of structure out of them. For the first few days after her husband's death, Josefina had believed anything and everything.

"I don't know why cancer is more respectable than masturbation," remarked Josefina.

"An illness makes us victims," answered Laura.

"Masturbation makes us guilty."

Laura laughed. She liked her open, honest laughter.

"I imagine a number of people must have started playing it safe now, after the funeral," continued Josefina. "The same thing happens with a heart attack; when someone they know has a heart attack, his friends and the people around him stop smoking, they're careful about the fatty foods they eat... That lawyer, in particular, is uncomfortable," she added. "As if he was always aware that his client died dressed like a woman, with broaches on his nipples and his head wrapped in a plastic bag."

"Do you mean Domínguez?" Laura asked. More than a question, it was an affirmation. "He doesn't lock himself up in a cubbyhole filled with metal hoops and three-pronged whips. He runs around after the secretaries in his office with his pants unzipped and a checkbook in his hand. Something absolutely vulgar," she asserted.

"How conventional," commented Josefina.

That business about Javier, on the other hand, brought out a sort of tenderness in her. It was rather childish, like an adolescent dream.

"Maybe we always have a child inside us, and we only let him out in private, when no one can see us," she said.

"A thirty-eight year old child who locks himself up with his favorite toy, far away from business affairs, from his family, and from any judgmental eyes," put in Laura.

"Something that my son might have thought of, not him," emphasized Josefina.

In her heart she held no rancor. Only a certain severity. A severity that had to do with the harshness of life.

"We women don't know what men want. Only another man can know that," she said.

"I don't think it's ignorance," replied Laura. "We simply don't want to know, so we can keep up the fiction about commonalities. They could be opposite, contradictory, irreconcilable desires. They could be insatiable, tenacious desires. Desires that are born from different bodies."

"Then... it's all hopeless," murmured Josefina.

"Not everybody ends up disastrously, suffocating themselves with a plastic bag," answered her friend. "There are always women who, for a little money, are willing to satisfy hidden desires. For the man who wants it, of course. Besides," she added, "I don't think men know what women desire."

"It seems to me that I don't care as much anymore," Josefina mused aloud. "What I mean," she explained, "is that now I don't have feelings just for Javier alone. Now what I care about is much more general," she concluded.

A few months after the death of her husband, Josefina found her son (who had just turned nine) playing with an orange in his mouth.

"Look, Mama, look," cried the boy. "I look like a little baby, breast-feeding," he said.

Josefina watched him.

"Keep doing it, over and over," she told him. "Do it whenever you feel like it."

This sanction that he hadn't asked for seemed to fluster Javier a little.

"So that you won't have to do it when you're thirty-eight years old, inside a plastic bag," she finished.

Javier kept sucking. It was true that his father had died, but he had a wonderful mother. After all was said and done, they were much better off by themselves.

# DESTRUCTION OR LOVE

I shop at a large department store on my street. It's well stocked, on its different floors you can buy everything you could imagine, from a box of pins all the way up to a motor-boat. I like to go there—the bottom floor has two entrances, from two different streets—and I carry a piece of paper in my pocket with a list of the things I need to buy for Ana's visit.

At first I thought it was a disadvantage for Ana and me to live in two different cities. Then I realized that it wasn't, that I liked longing for her when she was gone. We don't have any set dates for seeing each other. In fact, now that I think of it, I don't know anything about Ana's life. I only know that she lives in a far-off city, four hours away by air. I didn't want to ask for her phone number, but I gave her mine. Still, she doesn't use it. I just get a telegram from time to time that says: "Expect me on Thursday evening at eight o'clock. Ana." O.K. I think any word that doesn't have to do with desire is unnecessary, any extra information that adds nothing to our bodies and that could lessen the concentration on desire. Desire is demanding, it's intolerant, despotic. Desire doesn't want to know anything unless it has to do with bodies and expressions. I silently thanked her for never asking any question that didn't concern it. Why should she know where I work, whether I have any relatives, what my politics are or my favorite pastime?

She doesn't ask any questions. Neither do I. I don't

even know if Ana is her real name. Anyway, what does it matter? What does matter are the secret names we give each other, ones that don't appear on an I.D. card.

The telegrams arrive at all hours. Sometimes the doorman hands them to me, other times I get them by telephone. But the meetings are always at night. I'm grateful for that, because it allows me to prepare things in the morning.

On the appointed day I don't go to work. I give some reasonable excuse: I have a sore throat, my mother is sick, there's something wrong with the building's plumbing and I have to wait for the plumber. I couldn't simply say: "I'm busy. I have to get ready to meet Ana." It's never occurred to anyone to give somebody a day off for the most important reason in the world: a tryst. For illness, yes; for pleasure, no.

That's the least of my worries. The excuse always works, and I get up early, I drink a big cup of coffee, I light a cigarette and begin to imagine our rendezvous. Banal, everyday objects take on great importance then. Cigarettes, for example. I choose three and place them next to the bed: after we make love I like to put a cigarette— filter-tip down—into Ana's moist sex. The thin paper soaks up its fluid, and when I take it out of her vagina it has the flavor of the inner walls of her sex. I raise it to my lips, I light it—sometimes it's so damp that it's hard to light—and I take a deep drag. There's no cigarette that tastes better than that one. Its flavor has changed, mingled with her juices. Now it tastes a little like seaweed.

"Women smell like fish," my boss said one day when he was half drunk. We were having dinner. It was a business dinner, and he'd had too much to drink. He said it with a certain amount of disgust, as though he found the smell of fish disagreeable. And yet, I've seen him gulp down huge portions of sea-bass, oven-baked salmon, and turbots. I pointed that out to him, and he answered that the smell of fresh fish is one thing, but cooked fish is completely different. "Women smell like live fish," he said. It's a scent that excites me. I like strong scents, the kind they can't disguise or change. The fruits of the sea: hard crustaceans, pink shellfish, lustful oysters, eels as thin as serpents. A smell that stays on the hands, just like the odor of women. The powerful smell of cod between the legs. With my head plunged between Ana's thighs, I breathe in deeply. The oily vapor floods my lips, my chin, it goes into my nose, up to my head, and makes me dizzy. What do men like about women, if not their odor? I can understand perfectly how in ancient civilizations men would try to eat the bodies of their enemies. Love and hate can only end by swallowing the other. Don't pregnant women carry their child in their belly, among their entrails, mixed in with blood and water, in with fecal matter and alimentary bolus? They love their children because those children have been inside themselves, sucking on their secretions, getting nourishment from their glands, scrabbling in their starches and fats. That's what love is: a physiological matter, a question of entrails. I also understood the Japanese man who killed his girlfriend in Paris, cut her into little pieces and then stuck her in the freezer. Every day he would take a piece out of the refrigerator and eat it, seasoned with greens and condiments. A piece of arm in the oven, with tiny onions and peppers. For dessert, a breast, topped with cherry sauce. If women didn't give birth through their vagina—

103

which is a sort of defecation—they could vomit up their children. A convulsive, spasmodic vomiting that would throw out chunks of apple mixed with sperm, tears, a child's arm, neck bones, the gallbladder, the hairy head and the lungs.

The Japanese man gulped it down, and by doing so, he carried out an ancient ritual that has almost been forgotten: consumption through the mouth of what we love or what we hate, in order to possess it definitively. We also swallow cows in the form of filets, chickens in broth, white rabbits and partridges.

My desire for Ana is a corporal desire too, abundantly physiological. Her legs, for example: I love to shave them. I beg her not to wax them at home, but to come to me endowed with the hair that God has given her. I like her to come with all her things mixed with strong smells, hair, secretions and excrescences. She stretches out her legs on the black velvet sofa, raises her dress slightly, and I see her beautiful legs, her full, white thighs and her buttocks, covered with down, more abundant at its extremities, delicately fine, nearly imperceptible above the knees. Then I spread a sweet oil over her naked legs and I softly massage them. My fingers become saturated with the cream. Inner juices, physiological nectars, natural lubricants and herbal oils, who could tell them apart, and why should they?

Between one meeting and another, we are never in contact. She leaves the following morning, and I don't even go to the airport with her. Not a bit of the lukewarm farewells of lovers, the conventional goodbyes, the stupid conversations to fill time. Nothing of what the simple minded, the simpering, the wimpish call "love." But who would dare to say that we don't love each other? I feel an uncontrollable love for her cells. Those tiny cells, filled with cytoplasm and nucleus that make up her skin. I have examined them with a magnifying glass. Ana's epithelial tissue is arranged in small diamonds with delicate ridges whose sides touch. I think about her body: innumerable cells laid out along her femur, the nape of her neck, her throat, her clavicle, her tibia. It would add nothing to the minute knowledge I have of her skin, her muscles, her glands, to know where she lives, who her progenitors are, how much money she makes and what music she listens to when she's alone. Speaking of which: on today's list I included Bluebird by James Last. A plaintive flute, keen as a reed, that rends pleasingly. I had to go through several racks of discs to find it. No matter: the lover chooses the objects for the ritual of love with all the dedication and knowledge of a good collector.

I will wait for her with a dish of red strawberries that I'll make burst over her body so they'll bleed. Some of them will be the exact size of her clitoris. It will be like a homosexual act: clitoris against clitoris, the juice will spill around the swollen lips of her sex.

I spent some time at the department store in the section that carries different kinds of soap. Some are smooth, silky, of different colors, wrapped in cellophane. I pick out three: a green one that smells like pine, for the hair under Ana's armpits; a salmon color, for her sex; and lilac—the color they dressed witches in, before they burned them—for her back. I also buy a set of candles in the shape of water lilies, that float in a glass fountain filled with water, like a sea of sliced breasts. And the dark little balls of Iranian caviar that I like to place on her pubis, like

105

beetles entangled in its hair. To eat her up and to love her is one and the same. To fondle her and to savor her. My secretions mixed with hers, my sweat with her sweat, my bile with her bile, in the original chaos of earth, in the initial magma from which nothing was separable, solid from liquid, gases from viscera, skin from bones. It is born in turmoil and it dies in the worst of solitudes: that of a shattered body that no longer finds an echo in another body. I wonder if people die when they no longer have another body that responds to their own.

Yesterday my boss said—at a business lunch—that his marriage is a happy one, that his wife understands him. I laughed silently to myself. What's there to understand about that fat greaseball who gulps down enormous quantities of purified food—vegetable margarine, non-fat yogurt, dehydrated carrots—, who goes to the gym three times a week, and takes part in spiritual exercises once a year at some fashionable resort? I don't trust fat people: they turn their repressed drives into blubber. They sweat in the sauna and not in bed. I, on the other hand, am not fat: I would consider it offensive to the woman who loves me. Ana's hands, when they run along my side, have no difficulty in finding, under the texture of my skin, my firm bones. She touches them, pleasurably, she feels them, she differentiates them.

"I would eat up a good pot roast from your side," she tells me.

She licks my nipples and puts her tongue in my navel: the way animals lick each other, to heal their wounds or to show their affection.

While I wait for her, I leap around the living room like a chimpanzee, I beat my chest, I roar and walk on all fours. The animal inside me prepares for its feast. The other day I read in a magazine from the U.S. that it was a sort of therapy. I laughed. The Yankee psychiatrist who recommended those exercises thought he had discovered the prophylactic benefits of reverting, a few minutes a day, to being the animal we once were. When we forget that, we pay with our death: a bursting of the sickly viscera that speak through destruction, because they have been silent for so long.

I don't want Ana to die; I know that while we love each other with our primitive bodies, with the fat of her skin that protects her from cold, with the hairs of her nose that block the passage of bacteria, with the pulsing liver that filters out toxins, she will not die. Only bodies that have remained quiet for a long time die.

But one day she will marry. In her unnamed city, four hours away by air, she will walk down the aisle, the same way you come down with a disease. A social disease. Her body, bent over on itself; her viscera, in turmoil; her glands, swollen, will draw in to multiply— she, multiplied—in a child. A curious parthenogenesis, from which will emerge a second Ana, or an Angus, to carry on the destiny of the species. Being a man, I cannot divide myself, or multiply myself, or harbor another; I can only aspire, as a male, to swallow another body, to annihilate it: I have not been given the power of reproduction. I can only die or kill: only in that painful way can I be two-in-one.

Ana: *Word in Spanish, used to indicate that certain ingredients are to have the same weight or are to be of equal parts.*

Your name, then, is a mistake: we will never be

equal. We will love each other, nevertheless, in that difference, all the way to destruction. Which of the two of us will survive? You, to be able to give birth. Women stop being interested in men once they are pregnant. The intruder that we have injected in their viscera casts us out hopelessly: it separates us, it excludes us. We are all abandoned by a pregnant woman. That is why we turn toward other women, those who are not mothers, empty women who need to be filled. When you no longer return, I am certain to become depressed. Depression is not a sickness of the soul, as some believe: it is a sickness of the body that no longer desires, that does not know what to desire, that for some reason has been deprived of the object of its desire. Then, in not desiring, it slowly begins to destroy itself. My hair will no longer have a sheen: that sheen of desire; my body will become bent with age; my skin will take on the whitish tone of the dead that a mistaken civilization once considered superior; my hands will become numb, and my nose will no longer smell primordial substances in the turns of another's body. I will become old while you nurture your child: he will take away from me my sustenance.

But for that future enmity, there is still time.

I pick up the telephone and dial the number of the office. I ask for the boss. He does not answer immediately because he is a very busy man: he always has thousands of business matters to attend to, between one pill and the next (an anabolic steroid, a digestant, a pill for circulation of the blood, and anti-stress vitamins).

"This is Carlos," I tell him. "My head hurts, I'm feeling queasy…"

"Something you ate must have made you sick,"

said my boss, delighted to give me advice: "Take an Alka-Seltzer and get some rest. And above all, don't eat any solid foods for the rest of the day."

Solid food, I think: Ana's buttocks, with orange flambé.

"Right," I say, and hang up.

Or perhaps some dainty meninges in vinaigrette?

# INTERVIEW WITH THE ANGEL

I met the angel at a gay bar downtown. The bar was called Wilde's, and on the walls there were photographs of famous transvestites that I didn't recognize and had never seen, but who were undoubtedly highly appreciated figures in this gay-ambiance. I also learned that the term "gay-ambiance" was used precisely for those places where men and women got together to have a drink, laugh, feel blue, or hook up. Wilde's admitted both men and women, and the fauna on that July night had a very diverse look. It was a Friday, I think, and my woman had just left me. She can't stand it when I say "my woman," because when she mentions me she doesn't say "my man," but I feel ridiculous if I say "my companion," and it's only on formal occasions that I use the term "my wife". So anyway, "she" had just walked out on me, right then, in July, when so many things were closed, and the office where I work—a financial consulting firm—was on vacation. The one thing that's worse than a man's wife leaving him for another man, is when she leaves him for a woman. That's what had happened to me, and I wasn't able to digest it. It had settled itself in the middle of my stomach like a ball of cement, and it wouldn't let me swallow it or vomit it up, and at the same time it lay in the middle of my head, and I couldn't think of anything else, or even sleep. I didn't know if I needed to go to a psychiatrist, the courthouse or to a lawyer. I told her to go see a doctor, and that only brought an ironic little laugh and this biting remark:

"If I had known Irma before I met you, I certainly wouldn't have married you."

Irma was the name of my wife's lover; she was an interior designer, and she was very attractive. That was my first surprise: I was given to understand, or they made me believe, that lesbians were all ugly, mannish, losers, and it turns out that my wife had met up with a pretty lesbian, one with a profession, and who wasn't tied down. Obviously, I had either been given false information, or this woman was the exception. I told my wife not to rush into things, that there would be time for us to get a separation, a divorce, if that was what she wanted, and that in the meantime she should go see a doctor. I began to suspect that what was happening to my wife came from her not having had a child; that might explain everything.

"You're so vulgar," she answered.

We hadn't had a child, or a pair of them, for the simple fact that she had a retroverted uterus, which secretly pleased me, because the idea of being a father didn't exactly make me happy.

"What does she have that I don't?" I ventured to ask her before she left me.

What could a woman have that a man doesn't? When I really thought about it, I knew that I had some attributes that Irma was lacking, unless she got them at some sex-shop.

I suddenly realized that I was terribly interested in how two women made love. They had never taught me this in school or in my professional training, and during all

111

these years it had never even entered my mind, but now I realized that there was a hole in my knowledge. No, not a hole: a bottomless pit. There's one thing more insufferable than having a woman conspire against you, and that's having two women conspire against you. The bond that united them, whatever attraction they might feel for each other, was that they belonged to the same sex. This gave them an identity that was impossible for me. I would never be able to reach that unity, that complicity with anyone; I hadn't had it with her, I couldn't have it with another woman, and men didn't interest me. Or at least that's what I thought until I met the angel. What do we know about ourselves? A series of repeated actions or reflexes that can come apart at any minute like the vertebrae of a toy dinosaur. The angel was in the bar, drinking a glass of champagne and quietly talking to a man. He looked like a woman, but there was something in his build, in his shoulders, or perhaps in his voice that indicated a slight imbalance, an imperfection, the suspicion that something else was there. This bothered me, and aroused my curiosity. I thought of my wife, her feminine shape and full lips, at that very moment probably making love with another woman, and not with me, and it was not a happy thought. I could give her everything a man can give a woman, but Irma could give her something that I would never have or would never be: her essence as a woman. She had found the exact point to clip my wings, to humiliate me, to undermine me: something I couldn't change unless I went to Casablanca for an operation.

I spent the next ten minutes watching the angel. I feel a deep revulsion toward transvestites— and he was certainly one of them: their imitation of the ideal model is

112

so exaggerated that instead of a semblance, what they give you is a farce. The make-up, the powder, their gestures turn into a parody that separates them even further from the original.

At least, that's what I thought until I met the angel. It must have been the fact that I was half-scotched and profoundly affected by my wife's leaving that made me decide to go up to the bar with a devil-may-care attitude, holding a glass of gin, and with a certain aggressiveness that I undoubtedly thought was very masculine. I'm no expert in biology, but I was taught that we men are XY, and women are XX; the different chromosome gives us confidence in our strength, in our member. Until some woman leaves us for another woman and our whole world comes crashing down on us. What was I going to do with my chromosome that my wife didn't seem to need? I was half-smashed, and for me two women were XX and XX, a boring repetition, an unwavering symmetry.

I told the angel that my wife had left me for another woman. It was something that I definitely wouldn't have wanted to confess to a man (it would have felt like the undermining of my virility), but telling it to an angel gave me a sense of relief. The comfort of not knowing if I was talking to a man or a woman.

"Forget about chromosomes," the angel advised me. "That's certainly the last thing your wife and your wife's friend are thinking about."

There was my Y chromosome, cut loose, like a penis without an erection.

"I'm XY," I insisted. "She's XX." When I said "she," I was talking about my wife's lover, of course.

What is the sex of angels? This thought had

113

bothered me when I was a child, and now it was taking on unwonted currency.

"You—what are you?" I asked the angel rather aggressively.

I get aggressive when I'm confused, and lately almost everything was confusing me: my wife was cheating on me with another woman, I was in a transvestite bar, and the person I was talking to was either a guy or a girl—that was the unholy state of affairs.

"I'm whatever you want," the angel answered me in a natural tone of voice. "I'm your dream," he insisted. "If you want me to be a woman, I'll be a woman; if you want me to be a man, I'll be a man."

There's nothing worse than asking somebody what they want. It's a question without an answer. I knew what I wanted: for my wife to leave Irma, not to leave me; but as far as the angel was concerned, I had no idea what I wanted.

"And if you like, so you'll be completely satisfied," he added, "I'll be a man for a while, and then a woman."

But who in the world would ever get an idea like that? I like things to be straight and clear. I hate ambiguities.

"How can two women make love?" I asked him abruptly.

The angel laughed. He must have thought I meant the technique. I wasn't talking about that. I meant the kind of desire. There's nothing worse than loving someone whose desire eludes us. I wanted to understand my wife's desire.

"I think it's ridiculous," I added. "What could one

woman desire from another woman? They both have the same thing. I thought a person could only feel desire for something different."

"Could you be one of those people who think women are lacking something?" the angel said to me with an ironic smile.

"They have what they need to have," I answered assertively.

"And do you have what you need to have?" the angel questioned me, looking steadily at my fly.

I couldn't understand either, how, if the angel had the same thing I did, he might feel some sort of attraction to me. I wondered what the angel had.

"I have what I need to have," I declared firmly, even though I was feeling less and less sure of myself by the minute.

"To have something is an illusion, my dear," asserted the angel. "It's other people who decide what we have. That's why I offer a dream," he told me. "I'm what you decide I am: a man or a woman. I'm not the one who chooses: you are."

If what a person has is an illusion, someone else's fantasy, what was my wife's fantasy about Irma? When she shifted her desire someplace else, she deprived me of my sex.

"I can give you comfort," the angel told me. "If you need to believe that you are a real man, I'll get down in front of you on all fours so you can believe that you have what you want to have."

For a minute I thought: me, XY, with an erection, penetrating the angel's rosy orifice. But if that might get me back my sex—for myself, it didn't get it back to me—

as far as my wife was concerned.

"You have a fixed idea," the angel said to me. "All right: we all have fixed ideas. What would the world be like without fixed ideas. Nobody would build houses or put up factories or make movies. Similarities and differences are illusions too," he added. "To some, I sell the fantasy of similarity; to others, that of difference. In reality, I'm neither the same nor different. I am the very image of desire: evanescent, subtle, undecipherable."

"I like definite things," I answered. "Meals at certain times, making love in bed, getting paid at the end of the month."

"Your wife evidently got bored with that," remarked the angel.

What did my wife want? Did she even know, herself? Can anyone define their own desires? What did Irma have that I didn't? Or to put it another way, what did Irma not have that I did? It suddenly occurred to me that you could feel desire for someone because of what they're lacking, not because of what they have. I had another shot of gin, and I began to feel better. Now I began to see the angel in a more favorable light, the mouth distorted by lipstick, the visible hair of the armpits, the red dress that screamed to high heaven that it was a dress. There was no doubt, the angel was displaying too many female attributes for anyone to really believe he was a woman. I recalled that old proverb that says, "An illusion is what you think you have." And a movie called *To Have and To Have Not*. I looked over at the dance floor. A few couples were dancing, but I couldn't tell what sort of couples they were. The most I could say was that each couple was made up of two people, that's all.

"Desire is a fantasy," said the angel. "We all have various fantasies, and they change their shapes and sexes."

But my fantasy was my wife, and she was with another woman. Half drunk, I laughed at the fact that I had accepted the feminine gender of my rival: she was with another woman, not with another man. Was I the other woman's other man?

"Drink up," the angel told me. "You're learning too many things tonight."

I felt like punching him out. How dare somebody with a nebulous sex try to teach me? In the morning I was sure to have a hangover and my head would be clearer. But my wife wouldn't wake up beside me. My wife would wake up lying next to Irma. I thought of a terrible act of revenge: I would get into their apartment, I would open the bedroom door, and I would surprise them, lying in bed, naked, and I would kill them both. With a shot right through the neck of each of them. I would watch the red blood come pouring out of Irma and my wife, absolutely satisfied, like a sort of personal victory. While I was basking in the pleasure of this idea, another one suddenly crossed my mind: there I was, in bed with them, looking at them, watching them like a ravenous dog, trying to figure out the desire that each felt for the other. A desire that escaped me. A desire that I knew nothing about. A desire that excluded me. A repulsive desire that left me out in the cold. Would I feel less resentful if they gave me a place in it? But what place? As a spectator? The leftovers of their desire? I was getting boiling mad again, and I ordered another drink.

"Do you want to dance?" the angel asked me.

I rebuffed the invitation: I was afraid I would feel

ridiculous out in the middle of the dance floor, not knowing if the person I held in my arms was a man or a woman. There were couples like that, dancing. They didn't seem to care what other people thought of them; they were only interested in what their partner thought.

"This whole place has the feel of a ghetto." I told the angel.

"So do soccer teams, and the Army, and the Church, and political committees, and anti-alcohol societies," added the angel. "Not to mention couples," he finished. "Is there anything more like a ghetto than a family?"

I was a solitary type whose wife had left me, not finding anyone who was the same as I was or different from me. And so, a type without a ghetto. A rare and unique specimen.

"I can love you the way a man loves a woman, the way a woman loves a man, the way one man loves another man, the way two women love, or any other way you can think of," the angel offered me.

There's nothing worse than having to shape a desire, I thought. I didn't know what to choose. And besides, I didn't want to make a choice.

"It's fear of freedom," remarked the angel.

"All right," I admitted. "I don't want to be free. I want to have rules. I want to be told what I should desire."

"If you don't know what your desire is, I'll tell you," the angel said, trying to be helpful. "I'll be like an apparition. Vague and ambiguous, multiform, versatile."

"I'm afraid," I murmured, drunk as a child at a party.

"That's where desire begins," remarked the angel.

"In the place where there's fear, where nothing has a name and nothing exists: it only seems to."

I suddenly remembered something I had heard the priest say in religion classes: revelations are obscure. At the time it had sounded to me like a contradiction.

"Revelations are obscure," I told the angel, that night in July, when my wife left me. "Let's go," I added. I always had the excuse that I could say I was drunk.